POBBY AND DINGAN

Ben Rice was born in Devon in 1972. He read
English at Newcastle University and Oxford.
Ben won the 2001 Somerset Maugham Award.
He lives in London.

Ben Rice

POBBY AND DINGAN

VINTAGE

Thanks to Helen and Joe Stratford, Ridge rockhounds.
And to Craig Raine, Ian Jack and the brilliant friends who read drafts:
Rich Ager, Lucy Chandler, Helena Echlin, Ben Richardson, David Shelley,
Tim Robinson, Philip Traill.
Two publications were a source of information, *Australian Geographic*
and the pamphlet *Miner's Tales from the Black Opal Country* by
Rusty Bowen (1997).

Published by Vintage 2002

2 4 6 8 10 9 7 5 3 1

'Pobby and Dingan' first appeared in *Granta* in 2000;
'Specks in the Sky' first appeared in *The New Yorker* in 2001

Ben Rice has asserted his right under the Copyright, Designs
and Patents Act 1988 to be identified as the author of this work

Pobby and Dingan first published in book form in 2000 by
Jonathan Cape

Vintage
Random House, 20 Vauxhall Bridge Road,
London SW1V 2SA

Random House Australia (Pty) Limited
20 Alfred Street, Milsons Point, Sydney,
New South Wales 2061, Australia

Random House New Zealand Limited
18 Poland Road, Glenfield,
Auckland 10, New Zealand

Random House South Africa (Pty) Limited
Endulini, 5A Jubilee Road, Parktown 2193, South Africa

The Random House Group Limited Reg. No. 954009
www.randomhouse.co.uk

A CIP catalogue record for this book is available from the British Library

ISBN 0 09 928562 2

Papers used by Random House are natural, recyclable products
made from wood grown in sustainable forests. The manufacturing
processes conform to the environmental regulations of the
country of origin.

Typeset by Palimpsest Book Production Limited,
Polmont, Stirlingshire

Printed and bound in Australia by
Griffin Press

FOR MOLLIE

ONE

Kellyanne opened the car door and crawled into my bedroom. Her face was puffy and pale and fuzzed-over. She just came in and said, 'Ashmol! Pobby and Dingan are maybe-dead.' That's how she said it.

'Good,' I said. 'Perhaps you'll grow up now and stop being such a fruit-loop.'

Tears started sliding down her face. But I wasn't feeling any sympathy, and neither would you if you'd grown up with Pobby and Dingan.

'Pobby and Dingan aren't dead,' I said, hiding my anger in a swig from my can of Mello Yello. 'They never existed. Things that never existed can't be dead. Right?'

Kellyanne glared at me through tears the way she did the time I slammed the door of the ute in Dingan's face or the time I walked over to where Pobby was supposed to be sitting and punched the air and kicked the air in the head to show Kellyanne that Pobby was a figment of her imaginings. I don't know how many times I had sat at the dinner table saying, 'Mum, why do you have to set places for Pobby and Dingan? They aren't even real.' She put food out for them too. She said they were quieter and better behaved than me and deserved the grub.

'They ain't exactly good conversationists, but,' I would say.

And at other times when Kellyanne held out Pobby and Dingan were real I would just sit there saying, 'Are not. Are not. Are not,' until she got bored of saying, 'Are. Are. Are,' and went running out screaming with her hands over her ears.

And many times I've wanted to kill Pobby and Dingan, I don't mind saying it.

My dad would come back from the opal mines covered in dust, his beard like the back-end of a dog that's shat all over its tail. He would be saying, 'Ashmol, I sensed it today! Tomorrow we'll be on opal, son, and we'll be bloody millionaires! I can feel those bewdies sitting there in the drives, staring back at me. Checking me out. Waiting. They're red on blacks, Ashmol, I'll bet you anything! There's rumours going that Lucky Jes has taken out a million-dollar stone and a fossilised mammoth tooth with sun-flash in it. We're close, boy. Close. There's definitely something in that earth with the name Williamson on it!'

'Fairdinkum?'

His excitement always caught ahold of me. I would get a tingle down my neck and I would sit there with my ears pricking up like a hound's, my tongue hanging out, watching my dad's eyes darting around in his head. They were strange eyes – blue and green and with a flicker of gold in them. 'Eyes like opals,' my mum once said with a sigh, 'only a little easier to find.'

Well while Dad was pacing around the yard brushing himself off a bit and swigging from a stubby of V.B., Kellyanne would say, 'Dad, be careful! You almost trod on Pobby with your fat feet! Watch what you're doing!' But Dad would be too excited to do anything but say, 'Aw, sorry princess. Did I tread on your fairy-friends?' That was Dad. Me and him never took Pobby and Dingan seriously one bit.

But there were others who did. The older softer sort of folks in Lightning Ridge had sort of taken to Pobby and Dingan. They had totally given up throwing Kellyanne funny looks and teasing her about them. Now when she walked down Opal Street, some of the old-timers would stop and shout, 'G-day Kellyanne, g-day Pobby, and how's Miss Dingan doin' today?' It made you want to be sick all over the place. Lightning Ridge was full of flaming crackpots as far as I could see. It was like the sun had burnt out their brains. Now, I was as much a rockhound as the next kid, but I wasn't crazy enough to talk to imaginary friends, I'll tell you that for nothing. But one time Ernie Finch let Kellyanne enter Dingan in for the Opal Princess competition because Kellyanne had a cold. I'm not kidding. And the judges voted Dingan third place, and Nils O'Reiordan from the newspaper came and took photographs of Kellyanne with her arm around Dingan's invisible shoulder, and made out he was asking Dingan questions and everything. It was embarrassing. When the newspaper came out there was a picture of Kellyanne wearing a little silver crown over her long blonde hair, and underneath there was this sentence saying: *Two Opal Princesses — Kellyanne Williamson (aged eight) and her invisible friend Dingan who won third prize in this year's Opal Princess competition.* Plus every time we went to Khan's, Mrs Schwartz would hand my sister three lollies and say, 'There you go, Kellyanne. One for you, one for Pobby and one for Dingan. They look like they're both doing good.' Everybody knew everybody in Lightning Ridge. And some people even knew nobody as well, it seemed. Pobby and Dingan fit in to the little town just fine.

'Find anything today?' Mum asked one night when she'd got back from her job on the check-out at Khan's and me and Dad were relaxing after a hard afternoon's work out at the claim.

'Potch. Nothing special.'

'Nothing?'

I could see Kellyanne through the window over Dad's shoulder. She was sitting out back on a pile of stones talking to Pobby and Dingan, her mouth moving up and down, her hands waving around like she was explaining something to them. But all she was really talking to was the night and a few galahs. And if she was honest she would have admitted it there and then. But not Kellyanne.

'Where's my little girl?' Dad asked.

'Outside playing with some friends,' said my mum fixing my dad a look straight between the eyes.

'Pobby and Dingan?'

'Yup.'

My dad sighed. 'Jesus! That girl's round the twist,' he said.

'No she isn't,' said my mum. 'She's just different.'

'She's a fruit-loop,' I said.

'I kind of wish they were real friends, Mum,' Dad said. 'She don't seem to get on with the other kids around here too much.'

'What d'you expect?' said my mum, raising her voice and putting her hands on her hips. 'What d'you bloody expect when you drag your family to a place like Lightning Ridge? What d'you bloody expect to happen when you bring up an intelligent girl like Kellyanne in a place full of holes and criminals and freaks?'

'I still say Kellyanne could do with some real live mates,' went on my dad, as if he was talking to someone inside his beer.

Mum had stomped off into the kitchen. 'Maybe they *are* real!' she shouted back at him after rattling a few plates together. 'Ever thought about that, ye of little bloody imagination?'

My dad pulled a face. 'Who? Pobby and Dingan? Ha!' He drained his beer-can, positioned it standing up on the floor and then stamped on it until it was a disc of metal. Then he threw me a wink as if to say, 'Here comes the next wave of the attack, Ashmol!' And it came.

'Damn, Rex! You make me so bloody angry. Honestly! You haven't found any opal in two years. Not a glimpse of it. And opal's real enough for *you*. You don't stop dreaming about it and talking to it in your sleep like a lover! Well, as far as I'm concerned your bloody opal doesn't exist either!'

But that was a stupid thing for Mum to say, because the shops were full of opal and there were pictures of it everywhere and everybody was talking about it and the Japanese buyers forked out a whole heap of dollars for it. That's a fact. I saw them doing it with my own eyes out at Hawk's Nest.

Well, after my mum said this stuff about opal and after she'd done her usual piece about there being no money left in the tin under the bed, Dad sulked around a bit and kicked a few rocks around out in the yard. But then suddenly the door swung open and he came in full of energy like a new man and with a strange smile on his face. And what did he do? He started asking Kellyanne about Pobby and Dingan and how their days had been and what they were doing tomorrow. And he had never done that before in his life, ever. But he did it in a voice so you weren't too sure if he was joking around or not. Kellyanne was studying his face carefully, trying to work him out for herself. And so was I. And so was Mum. And then Dad asked Kellyanne if he could run Pobby and Dingan a bath. And he asked straight-faced and honest-sounding and Kellyanne eventually said yes that was all right, but only she was allowed to dry them after it.

I said, 'Dad, what the hell are you doing? You know all that Pobby and Dingan stuff's just horseshit! She'll never grow out of it if you talk like that!'

And Dad answered, looking at his feet, 'No, Ashmol. I think I've been unfair on Pobby and Dingan. I think that they do exist after all! I just haven't, like, recognised it until now.'

He grinned and rubbed his hands together and disappeared into the bathroom to run the taps while Kellyanne stood there glowing with pride and flashing me a smile from the doorway which made me feel sick. I looked at Mum, but she had a contented look on her face and started setting about making tea and bickies. I sat at the table feeling like someone had marooned me on a desert island.

Well, I don't like thinking about it, but from that moment on my dad became a total dag. Now when he got up in the morning and woke up Kellyanne for school he would wake up Pobby and Dingan too. Yes, he would. He started talking to them like they was real people. And he wasted all kinds of money on buying them birthday presents too – good money that could have gone into a better generator if you ask me. Oh, yes, Dad had himself some fun by going along with the Pobby and Dingan thing. One time he even took Kellyanne, Pobby and Dingan out to the Bore Baths in the ute. When I ran out to join them with my towel around my shoulders, my dad shouted, 'Sorry, son. Can't take you today, Ashmol. Not enough room with Pobby and Dingan in here.' He waved out of the window with a big smile on his face and drove off thinking he was a funny kind of bloke. Sometimes Mum would ask him to come and help with the washing up. But no! Dad was helping Pobby and Dingan get dressed or helping them with their homework. Kellyanne loved it. But Mum went a bit strange. I don't think she could decide if she was angry or pleased that Dad had become mates with Pobby and Dingan. And I think even Kellyanne began to realise pretty soon that Dad was only doing it to get back at Mum for having a go at him or something. He wasn't a very subtle sort of bloke, my dad, when it came down to it. He drank too much for a start and spent too much time underground in the dark.

TWO

When Dad left for the claim one morning he volunteered to take Pobby and Dingan with him to get some exercise while Kellyanne was at school. He was trying to separate her from them, I suppose, now I think about it. Kellyanne's teachers, you see, had complained that she wasn't concentrating in class and was always talking to herself and hugging the air. Well, I got to admit it was a funny sight seeing my dad heading out holding hands with two invisible people. Kellyanne watched him, making sure he helped them up into the cabin of the ute and then Dad started the car up and waved out of the window and made out he was fastening Pobby and Dingan's seat-belts.

'Don't worry, princess!' he shouted. 'I'll look after them while you're at school and make sure they don't get up to no mischief. Won't I, Pobby? Won't I, Dingan?'

I was getting a bit worried. My dad was turning into a poof. And the neighbours were talking about him walking alone and talking to himself and things like that. They said he was even drunker than normal.

That same night Mum still wasn't back from work and

Dad had swallowed a few beers too many shall we say. He was singing 'Heartbreak Hotel', and doing a sort of Elvis dance. I knew he had forgotten to bring back Pobby and Dingan from the claim, but I didn't say a word. I wanted to see what Kellyanne would have to say about it, so I just sat there playing on my Super Mario with its flat batteries, hoping Kellyanne would come in from the kitchen and get all ratty. Dad sat down and started talking about how he had been up at the puddling dam doing a bit of agitating. He told me that today Old Sid the Grouch had found traces of colour within twenty metres of his claim. I said, 'Do your Elvis dance again, Dad, it's really cool.' Of course it wasn't cool at all, but I wanted to keep him from thinking about his day. He might have remembered about Pobby and Dingan in the nick of time. Luckily he didn't and Kellyanne came rushing in from the kitchen where she was having a go at cooking yellowbelly from Mum's instructions.

'Dad. Where's Pobby and Dingan? Where are they?' she cried, all anxious.

'Now you're in for it, Dad,' I said. 'Better make something up quick.'

Dad's face suddenly flushed all kinds of colours. He swivelled around and spilt some beer on the floor. 'Hi, princess! Relax now, darl. Pobby and Dingan's right here sittin' on the couch next to Ashmol.'

Kellyanne looked over at the couch. 'No they're

not, Dad,' she said. 'They hate Ashmol. Where are they really?'

'Oh no, that's it,' said my dad. 'I completely forgot. They're out in the back yard watering the plants.'

Kellyanne ran outside. She came back looking pale. 'Dad, you forgot all about Pobby and Dingan, didn't you? You've lost them, haven't you?'

'No, princess,' said my dad. 'Calm down, sweetheart. They were in the ute with me when I came back.'

'I don't believe you,' said Kellyanne, tears growing out of her eyes. 'I want you to take me out to the claim to look for them right now.' That was my sister! She was mad as a cut snake.

'Christ, Kellyanne!' I said. 'Grow up, girl!'

Dad looked a bit desperate. 'Aw, princess, come on, now. I'm busy having a brew and a chat with Ashmol. Are you sure your little friends aren't here?'

'Positive,' said Kellyanne, wiping her eyes on her sleeve.

And so Dad couldn't do nothing except take Kellyanne out to the claim called Wyoming where he had his drives.

'You come too, Ashmol,' Dad said.

'No thanks,' I said, folding my arms across my chest. 'Count me out. No bloody way is Ashmol Williamson going looking for two non-existent things.'

But in the end I went along all the same, making

sure I did lots of tutting and shaking my head.

When we arrived at the claim the two of them walked around calling out, 'Pobby! Dingan! P-P-P-Pobbbbby! Where are you?' I sat firm on a mullock heap and opened up a can of Mello Yello. I knew what my dad was thinking. He was thinking that any minute now Kellyanne was going to suddenly imagine she had found her imaginary friends and start beaming all over her face. But she didn't. She kept calling out and looking real worried. She ran around the four corners of the claim looking from side to side. Pobby and Dingan were nowhere to be seen, she said. And who was going to argue with her? Dad wasn't. And I was having shit-all to do with it.

They looked behind the mullock heaps and they looked in the old Millard caravan where we used to live when we first came out to the Ridge, and they looked behind the mining machinery and behind a clump of leopard gums. And I'll bet all the time my dad was thinking: I must be going hokey cokey. If the other miners could see me now! Dad knew pretty darn well, you see, that only Kellyanne was going to find Pobby and Dingan. He would just have to wait until she did. Or maybe he was secretly hoping that this was Kellyanne's little way of putting her imaginary friends behind her for good. Anyway, he kept throwing desperate glances my way and shouting over, 'Come on, Ashmol, lend a frigging hand, will you?' But I wasn't budging, and so eventually Dad sat down exhausted by the hoist where the huge blower was curled up like a snake and just called out, 'Pobby! Dingan! Listen! You two! I'm sorry I didn't look after you proper! I'm sorry I left you out here! I've got some lollies in my pocket if you want some!' That was a fat lie. He never had any lollies.

Well in the last hour before dark Dad pulled himself off his backside and looked real hard. You had to hand it to him. He got down on his knees and crawled around in the dirt. He rummaged through piles of rocks. He looked behind trees, in front of trees, up trees and down trees. He crossed over on to the next claim which was owned by Old Sid the Grouch. He shouldn't of. But he did. He searched like he was mad, and there was sweat slipping down his cheeks. He worked harder than he ever mined in his life, I reckon. And it was hard to believe he was searching for Nothing. Diddlysquat. Stuff-all. And then there was a piece of very bad timing.

Old Sid, who lived out there in a camp made out of pieces of corrugated iron, came running out from behind a weeping wilga tree and stood by the starpicket at the corner of our claim with his arms folded. He had a big grey moustache, and he wore this kind of stupid beany hat that made him look even meaner and stupider than he was. And believe me that was stupid. The rumour was he ate frill-neck lizards on toast for breakfast.

Old Sid watched as my dad got down on all fours and leant over the hole of Old Sid's mine shaft and called out, 'Pobby and Dingan! You down there?' Sid couldn't make head or tail of what was going on. He thought my dad was ratting his claim and stealing all his opal. He shouted out, 'Hey! You! Rex Williamson! What the hell you doin' on my claim?'

My dad turned around, startled. He was totally off his guard. He began to go red and get all embarrassed and then he started trying to make up some sort of story about looking for his watch, but then he changed it halfway into a lost-cat story – but he stuttered over that too and so he got back down on his knees and started spinning some yarn about looking for one of his contact lenses. It all went a bit wrong. My dad wasn't much good at lying.

'You been drinking, Rex?'

I walked up to Sid to put things straight.

'My dad ain't been drinking nothing, Mr Sid,' I said. 'You see, my sister's got two imaginary friends called Pobby and Dingan – maybe you've heard of them – and she thinks my dad lost them out on the claim. And we're here looking for them. Sounds strange, I know – but there you go, that's the truth of it.'

Sid looked totally baffled and pretty angry. He said, 'Now don't you go making excuses for your old man, Ashmol Williamson! You may be a clever kid, but your daddy's been ratting my claim, ain't he? Some of us miners have been suspecting him for some time. But now here's the proof of it! And you're just trying to stick up for him, ain't you?'

My dad stumbled over to Old Sid with his fists clenched. He said, 'Now look here, Sid. I ain't been ratting nothing. I ain't no thief. I'm looking for my daughter's imaginary friends and you'd better bloody well believe it, mate!'

But Sid wasn't having any of it. 'You can talk about invisible people as much as you like, Rex Williamson,' he said. 'But I've had my doubts about you. A lot of us have. I've already reported you to the mining authority, and as soon as I saw you on my claim this evening, snuffling around for my opal, the first thing I did was radio the police, and, as a matter of fact, here they are right now!'

The noise of a car drove into our ears and a four-wheel-drive police jeep came wobbling down the creamy red track that leads to our claim. It pulled over by our old Millard caravan and out came two policemen. Bulky fellas with hats and badges and shit. I was getting a bit worried. Kellyanne was still looking around the claim for Pobby and Dingan, and Dad had started shouting about how dare Old Sid call him a ratter, he who'd worked honestly for God knows how long, and been a pretty good sort of bloke all round. And then I went up to one of the police blokes and told him the truth of the matter about Pobby and Dingan and what my dad was doing on Old Sid's claim. But I hadn't got too far when there was this noise of scuffling and a grunt and I turned around to see that my dad had lost his cool and snotted Old Sid one in the nose. Well, after that the police were on my dad in a flash, and they had him in handcuffs and everything. Kellyanne came running over in a panic, saying, 'Leave my dad alone! Leave him alone!' But Dad was bundled into the car and driven away. And it was us who were left alone. And then Kellyanne sat down on a mullock heap and broke down in sobs, for I reckon it was a bit too much to cope with, losing two imaginary friends and one real dad in an afternoon.

For a while I didn't know what to do. I just stood there watching one of those fluffy roly-poly things go cartwheeling over the claim on a breath of wind. And I thought about my dad and what a tangle he'd got himself into. And then I said, 'Kellyanne, come on, we'd better get home. Pobby and Dingan will come back tonight on their own and Dad will be fine as soon as this is sorted out and the police realise what he was doing on Sid's land. Come on, we'll walk back and tell Mum, and get the bad bits over and done with.'

But Kellyanne didn't stop looking worried. She legged it over to the mine shaft and stepped over the tape which was around the top of the hole to stop people going down. She got down on all fours and peeked over the edge. And she called out Pobby and Dingan's names down the mine shaft. There was no reply of course. She stayed there on all fours looking down that shaft for half an hour.

'This just isn't like them,' she said. 'This is not like them at all.'

While Kellyanne was doing this I walked over to Old Sid the Grouch who was still watery-eyed with pain and holding on to his nose and mooching around his claim checking to see if all his opal dirt was still there. I said, 'You've made a big mistake here, Mr Sid. We Williamsons were just looking for my sister's imaginary friends. We ain't no ratters.'

Old Sid spat on the ground and said something about our family needing our heads inspected, and how my poor mother was too much of a pom for this place, and how he felt sorry for us that our dad was a ratter, and how the rumour was my dad had come to the Ridge in the first place to hide away from the Law. And I felt so angry I walked right away, pulled Kellyanne up by the arm and marched her home. It took an hour and a half, and all the way Kellyanne was whining about how she'd lost Pobby and Dingan, and how she wouldn't be able to sleep or eat until she found them, and how if they'd been here then they could have saved Dad and none of this would have happened. Her worried little face was covered in white dust so she looked like a little ghost.

Well, it was dark when we got back to our home, and

my mum had already heard what had happened from the police and she sent us to bed and said not to worry because everything would be sorted out soon. But I never saw her looking so angry and panicky and unsorted-out in her life. And her bedroom light stayed on all night, I swear.

And that night at around twelve was when Kellyanne crawled into my bedroom through the Dodge door which I'd got Dad to fix up to make going to bed more interesting. And my sister looked at me all pale and fuzzy-faced and said, 'Ashmol! Pobby and Dingan are maybe-dead.' And she just sat there in her pyjamas all nervous and hurt. But I was half-thinking of Dad and if he was in prison and how the whole thing was Pobby and Dingan's fault. And then I tried to get my head round how it could be their fault if they didn't even exist.

And I fell asleep thinking about that.

THREE

When I woke up the next day, Mum told me how Dad had been in prison overnight but he was being released and sent home until there was a trial or something which would prove that Dad hadn't been ratting Old Sid's claim. Mum was pretty frantic with worry though, and she said Dad would have to keep a low profile in the Ridge and stay at home awhile until the whole thing had blown over and he'd got his respect back among all the miners and stuff. Ratting, you see, is the same thing as murder in Lightning Ridge – only a bit worse.

We waited for him to come home and played a game of chess to help pass the time and calm each other down. I got Mum in checkmate after fifteen moves. No one can beat me at chess, and I reckon one day I'll be a bloody grandmaster or something. Either that or a secret agent like James Blond. But I have to admit that this time Mum wasn't concentrating too well and so she made it pretty easy for my bishops and knights to do the business. The problem was that Mum kept gazing out of the window with a dazed look about her, and I was pretty sure she wasn't just thinking about Dad but she was also pommie-sick again and thinking about Granny Pom and the other pommie friends she left behind her in England all those years ago.

Anyway, when Dad eventually came home late that afternoon he gave us all a hug and said that the prison was OK and a bit like a motel except that the beds were hard and the bars weren't the kind that served beer. He said not to worry because he was going to sort out this whole mess good and proper. But he didn't know quite how. And Mum told him he'd better not try and sort out anything but just keep his head down and keep out of trouble until the trial and all that shit. And then my dad asked me if Pobby and Dingan had come back yet. I shook my head. 'Kellyanne thinks they are maybe-dead,' I said.

'She's still very upset,' said my mum. 'She's been sulking all day. You shouldn't have been so careless Rex, you really shouldn't.'

'I shouldn't have done a lot of things,' said my dad, letting out a long sigh. But he was pleased to be back. And he was glad I think of all the attention we were giving him. I even went and got him a stubby of V.B. from the fridge and then I sat there asking him more things about prison. And after that we talked about opal all day until it got dark and until there was suddenly this godawful shriek and Mum came rushing in from near the front door saying, 'Oh, my Lord! God! Help! Get water!

Get water fast!' She ran into the kitchen and started filling up a bucket from the sink.

We rushed out front and what hit me first was a smoky smell like the smell of a cigar. And then when I peered out into the dark I could see grey figures twisting up into the sky quite awesomely. Dancing. But my dad whispered, 'Jesus! They've set our fence on fire!' And then I twigged that those figures were swirls of smoke, and some of the stakes were actually flaming at the tops. The light from the flame danced against the walls of our little house and showed up enormous dark lines like zebra stripes. They were letters sprayed on with an aerosol can or something, and they said:

BURN THE RATTERS

Mum threw her bucket of water over the fence post while I ran in to fill up some more and Dad just stood gaping at the words on the wall beside the living-room window. He was there when I came back, still staring, his hand on the back of his neck, not saying a word. And then he disappeared around the back of our house for paint. When the flames were out I went in to Kellyanne's room and told her what had happened. But she just hid under her blanket and said nothing.

FOUR

About this time Kellyanne started getting really sick. I can't explain it and neither could anybody else. She just lay in bed saying she was very tired and worried because Pobby and Dingan hadn't come back, and that she couldn't be sure if they were dead or not. They might still be wandering around over the opal fields all lost and frightened, and there were wild pigs out there and snakes and all kinds. It made her want to puke just to think about it. Well Pobby and Dingan had got us into enough shit as it was thank you very much, and I felt angry with them. Pretty goddamn angry for spoiling our family name. And I thought Kellyanne was faking at first, pretending to be ill like she pretended to have friends. But then I heard her puking in the dunny. She *was* sick. She really was.

She wouldn't eat anything. Mum called Jack the Quack and he came and sat on Kellyanne's bed and did some stethoscope stuff. He told my mum that Kellyanne was suffering from a nervous illness or depression, and that she had a fever. He tried to persuade her to eat a little of something. But she wouldn't. He told Kellyanne that if she kept this up he would have to take her to hospital and force-feed her through some disgusting pipes. I told Jack about everything that had happened with Pobby and Dingan but he just smiled and frowned and smiled again and used the words 'syndrome' and 'clinical' and 'psychological' a lot. Well I didn't know what those words meant but they sounded like pretty useless kinds of words to me.

Before Jack the Quack left he hung around talking to Dad about his new jackhammer. He told him he'd heard about the scuffle out at the claim and that he was behind Dad all the way – and didn't believe a word of the rumours that were spreading around Lightning Ridge like a bushfire. But there was something funny about how Jack the Quack was behaving. Sort of nervousish. And when he said Kellyanne would be better off in hospital, I reckoned he said that because he didn't trust my folks to look after her. Plus, when Mum asked him to stay for dinner he made some excuse about having to go line-dancing and scuttled away like a goanna.

My dad started to look pale too. He said, 'No bastard's taking my princess to no stupid hospital,' over and over again. 'We Williamsons can look after each other just fine. We don't need no charity or help from nobody!' Late at night he would pace up and down, shaking his head saying, 'You're right, Mum. This is all my fault. Maybe we should never have come out to the Ridge in the first place. She's a sensitive kid. Too precious for this place. She gets bullied at school, don't she?' That was my dad. He started to get all emotional, and began working his way through a slab of V.B. And then he cried. It was like the beer was going in his mouth and coming out of his eyes.

Well, Mum and Dad didn't dare tell Kellyanne to stop this once and for all or explain to her straight that Pobby and Dingan were only in her imagination and that she'd better switch the bloody thing off. They'd done it once before, you see, and Kellyanne went a little bit crazy and started screaming so hard the whole town thought they was being air-raided by nuclear missiles from France. They knew better than to tell my sis that she was being stupid. Kellyanne didn't handle that kind of criticism stuff too well.

So now Kellyanne just lay in bed. She slept or just lay whimpering. That's all that she did. She got so thin that it didn't look like there was any kind of body under the sheet.

Well, all this started to rattle my mind, and every day I would wriggle through the car door and clamber up on to my bunk and sit thinking. I figured this was the end of the world because we were all going crazy. Pobby and Dingan were messing up my family and they weren't even here. And they also weren't even anywhere. And although I thought my sister was nuts, I didn't like to see her like this and hear her chucking up in the dunny.

And I wanted my dad to cheer up and go off to his mining again, and I wanted my mother to stop worrying and being homesick, and I wanted the Williamson family name to gleam and sparkle and be all right.

And I knew flaming well that the answers to all these problems lay with Pobby and Dingan themselves.

And then I figured out something else. I didn't like to admit it, but it seemed to me the only way to make Kellyanne better would be to find Pobby and Dingan. But how do you go looking for imaginary friends? I stayed awake all the bastard-night trying to get my head around the problem. I reckoned that the first thing would be to have as many people as possible looking for them, or pretending to look, so that at least Kellyanne knew people cared, that they believed in her imaginary friends and wanted to help out. See, I'd remembered that Kellyanne was always most happy when people asked questions about Pobby and Dingan. Usually that made a smile crawl over her face. And it seemed to me if a hell of a lot of people was asking questions about them then she would get better fast. I also knew darn well that there was quite a few people in the Ridge who loved Kellyanne to bits even though they were a little unsure about the rest of us Williamsons, and there were some who almost believed in Pobby and Dingan or who were real nice and understanding about it. And I had it in the back of my mind that if those people believed in imaginary friends and all that shit, or if they knew how real those friends were for Kellyanne, then they'd believe that my dad really had been looking for them out at the mine and not ratting Old Sid's claim.

The two problems seemed to go together somehow.

So this is what I did. The next day I went around town calling in at the shops and telling people why Kellyanne was sick. I went to the Wild Dingo, and even to The Digger's Rest where the toughest miners drink. I said, 'Howdy, I'm Ashmol Williamson, and I've come to tell you my dad's no ratter and my sister's sick cos she's lost her imaginary friends.' Well there was a silence and then one of those miners came up to me, grabbed my collar and held me up by it, so that my feet came off the ground. He pulled me so close I could smell his stinking breath and said, 'Listen here, kid. You go back and tell your daddy, if he ever shows his face in here again *he's* gonna be the *imaginary one*. Understand? Imaginary! Geddit? Dead!' Well, I was just about to shit myself when a bunch of other miners came over and said to the bloke, 'Put the kid down, mate. Rex Williamson is a friend of mine and those kids of his are good kids.' Well this bastard threw me on the floor and said, 'You wanna watch who your friends are!' to the men, and then walked out. The group of miners picked me up, brushed me down and asked if I was OK. I told them yes, but I was a little bit worried about my sister Kellyanne because she was really sick and might get taken away to hospital, and how I was gonna try and lick clean my dad's name until it shone red on black.

I had a busy day, allrighty. I went to the Bowling Club to tell the pokie players and also to the Wallangalla Motel where there was some line-dancing practice going on. You should of seen me. I tried to go up to people on the dance floor and get them to stop dancing and listen, but they were too busy doing their moves to the music and I kept getting caught up between people's arms. In the end I just walked up to the bloke with the tape decks and grabbed the microphone and shouted, 'Ladies and gents! Sorry to interrupt your dancing, but my name's Ashmol Williamson, and my sister is sick and we need to help her find her imaginary friends tomorrow morning!' There was this nasty high-pitched screech from the microphone, like it didn't exactly enjoy what I'd said, and then everyone, about fifty people in all, stopped dancing and turned around to look at me all at once. There was a silence and then I heard people mutter my dad's name and whisper the word 'ratter' to each other, and some of them frowned at me, and I knew all of a sudden what it feels like to be a mosquito. Well, I coughed into the microphone and explained in a shaky voice about my sister and Pobby and Dingan and how my dad got into trouble on Old Sid's claim. And I told them how Pobby and Dingan had liked nothing better than line-dancing, and that unless we found them they might never be able to do it ever again. And then I suddenly ran out of things to say and felt a bit weird with all those lines of people looking at me, so I just put down the microphone and ran out and got back on my Chopper and pedalled off wobbly-legged.

I went almost everybloodywhere. I went to the Automobile Graveyard and spoke to Ronnie who recognised me from the time he gave me the cool door off the Dodge. I went out to the camps at Old Chum and Vertical Bill's and the Two Mile. And some people whispered to each other about Dad and some didn't. And some folks thought I was nuts. And some were nuts themselves anyway so it didn't make no difference. I even went out and told the tourists out at The Big Opal. They patted me on the head and smiled and whispered to each other in funny languages. One big American man filmed me with his video camera and told me to say something cute into it so he could show his friends back home. But when it came to the crunch I couldn't say anything and I didn't feel too much like smiling. So I showed him my James Blond double-o-seven impression where I turn sharp and fire a gun like on the video that my friend Brent's parents gave him after they struck opal out at the Three Mile. And I told this tourist how when I grew up I might have a James Blond gun and everything. But then I realised I was wasting time and Kellyanne was sick, and my dad was being called a ratter, and these tourists wouldn't really give a shit, but.

I went out to the town hall where some of the black kids were practising a traditional Korobo-something dance with their teacher in funny outfits and didgeridoos and drums. I stood there for a while and watched them and had a good laugh at how dumb they looked. And then one of them started running straight at me with a spear and told me he was going to shove it up my ass unless I dooried right off out of the hall. But the teacher stopped him and honked on her didgeridoo and told him to shut up and get back to doing his hunting dance. But before they started the dance I managed to squeeze in a few words about how sick Kellyanne was, and I also asked them if maybe they could do a dance to conjure up Pobby and Dingan some time tomorrow. And the teacher said that they would certainly think about it if they had time, and then she started going off on one about how her ancestors believed opals were dangerous and stuffed full of evil spirits, and how maybe my family was paying the price for worshipping it and drilling horrible holes in the beautiful aboriginal land.

Well, I'd had enough of hearing this goddamned hooey, as my dad called it, and so I shot off and cycled out on the dirt roads around about a couple of hundred more camps on my rusty old Chopper bike telling people about Kellyanne and how she was ill because of losing her imaginary friends. It was a hot day, and hard work, and so I made sure I was tanked up with Mello Yello to stop my mouth getting dry from all that explaining I was doing. When I told people what had happened to my sis, some of them looked at me like I was a total fruit-loop. But a lot of them already knew about Pobby and Dingan because they had kids who went to the same school as Kellyanne out at Walgett and they had seen her talking to them on the old school bus. One older girl out at the caravan park came up to me and said, 'Are you Kellyanne Williamson's brother? My mum says you Williamsons are stupid people and your dad's a drunk ratter and so you better go away or I'll punch you the way I punched your sister that time at the Bore Baths.' I gave her the finger and pedalled off fast cos she was too big for me. But she called after me, 'The only friends you Williamsons have are imaginary ones! Just you remember that, Ashmol Williamson!'

But some people were real nice about it. On one of the camps a woman gave me a Mello Yello and a cake and asked me how my mum was going at the supermarket. She said, 'The sooner they get your pretty little sister to hospital the better.' I answered, 'Yup. But it's more complicated than that, Mrs Wallace. See, Kellyanne's sick-with-worry sick; she ain't hospital-sick sick.' I also met this kid who knew as much about Pobby and Dingan as I did. He said he didn't like Kellyanne too much but he thought Pobby and Dingan were all right. He said he had a much better imaginary friend than Kellyanne. It was a giant green ninja platypus called Eric. He didn't talk to it, but.

One twinkly and crazy old timer with a parrot took me into the bust-up old tram where he lived and told me he had heard Kellyanne talking to Pobby and Dingan once when she was at the town goat races. She had been standing with three lollies on Morilla Street. This old miner said he believed that Pobby and Dingan really existed and he would look out for them as carefully as he could when he was walking around town. He would also check in at Steve's Kebabs to see if they'd stopped by for a feed, and he would write a poem called 'Come Home My Transparent Ones!' and hand it around his bush poet mates. This old codger didn't seem to understand that I just wanted him to pretend to be looking for Pobby and Dingan. But there you go.

I stayed out till dark explaining to all these Lightning Ridge families how tomorrow morning they had to go out along Opal Street and the dirt roads and make a big show of looking for Pobby and Dingan so that Kellyanne could see that people really cared about them. And I did some explaining about what had happened to my dad and what a mix-up there had been. And how Pobby and Dingan weren't real but Kellyanne thought they were and that's what counts, and how my dad wasn't a ratter but people thought he was and that's what counts too. Some of the people were real nice about it and gave me some bags of Twisties, and I went around munching them and putting up signs I had made saying:

LOST! HELP!
KELLYANNE WILLIAMSON'S FRIENDS POBBY AND DINGAN.
DESCRIPTION: IMAGINARY. QUIET.
REWARD IF FOUND.

And I put on the address of our house and tacked the notices up on telephone poles and walls and machinery and shit. When I cycled home I watched people looking at the notices, and I saw that some of them had been graffitied over with the word 'Ratter', but I also noticed that a lot of them hadn't been. Well, that was a good sign. And a lot of folks were smiling and laughing. I went to bed that night pretty full of myself for having had a go at least at clearing my family name and standing up for everybody. And I hadn't got beaten up or anything, either – which was cool.

Well, Kellyanne wasn't getting any better and she wasn't saying anything except muttering the names of Pobby and Dingan, and Mum and Dad were spending all their time by her bedside taking her temperature and telling her everything was going to be all right and making her soup which she never ate. And Dad was still pacing up and down clutching at this letter from the hospital which said Kellyanne had to go there immediately, and that they needed to do some tests. My folks, I reckon, were beginning to think hospital was the only way out.

When the blanket everybody calls night was tucked in all snugly over Lightning Ridge I stayed in my room and hung my head out of the window and said a sort-of-a-prayer. I said something like: 'Please let people go looking for Pobby and Dingan tomorrow!' And I squeezed my hands together. When I'd finished the prayer, I realised I hadn't put no address on it, and I was just whispering, 'P.S. This prayer is for God or anyone powerful who can hear me,' and wondering if it wouldn't be better to pray to someone cooler like James Blond, when I was distracted by the sound of Mum and Dad shouting at each other in their bedroom. And I only caught a few words because it sounded muffled like they was shouting with bits of cake in their mouths. But I heard Mum say she was tired a lot and homesick for England and Granny Pom and fed up of working at the check-out at Khan's and not being able to look after her family for herself. And then I heard my dad shouting something about Her Royal Highness, and he kept repeating a man's name, but I can't remember what it was exactly. Probably some bloke who'd called Dad a ratter again and got him all upset and irritable.

FIVE

The next day I got up early, gobbled my breakfast, attached bits of cardboard to my spokes with clothes-pegs and rode into town in fourth gear sounding like a motorbike. There was a stream of trucks driving out to the mines, and the sounds of drilling rigs in the distance. It seemed like the whole town was mining as usual. But then, just as I was going down Opal Street I saw that there was a bunch of people crouched down on the roadside looking under trees and cars and over fences and everything. When they saw me riding by on my souped-up Chopper, one of them saluted me like I was some sort of general and shouted out, 'Young Ashmol! Go tell Kellyanne we're searching as hard as we can!' I almost fell off my bike with surprise. The first part of my plan had worked. People were actually looking for Pobby and Dingan, they really were! I pedalled home like a maniac to tell my family.

When Dad heard what I'd gone and done he patted me on the head and said, 'Good thinking, son.' I told him it was important that Kellyanne saw what was taking place and Dad managed to persuade her to get out of bed. He lifted Kellyanne up in her sheet and took her out to the ute. Mum drove because Dad still wasn't comfortable about going out and being seen by people yet.

I sat in the back watching everything, and when I got into town I made Mum pull over so Kellyanne could see the special notices I had put up on the fences and gates and trees. She smiled a little when she saw them. I said, 'Sorry, Kellyanne. I didn't know how to describe them proper. I mean, what do they look like?' And Kellyanne whispered that they didn't look like anything in particular, but Dingan had a lovely opal in her bellybutton, only you had to be a certain kind of person to see it. And Pobby had a limp in his right leg.

There were a few more people on the dirt roads, and people out with their dogs, and we pulled up alongside them and waved out of the windows. They came up to the ute and said, 'Hey, Kellyanne, we've been looking for six hours now and we're not giving up until we find Pobby and Dingan. So don't worry your head about it.' My sis smiled weakly. One boy asked her, 'Do Dobby and Pingan speak Australian?'

'No,' said my sis. 'They speak English quietly. And they likes to whistle. But you have to be a certain kind of person to hear them.' It was the first time Kellyanne had done this much speaking for a long while and it brought a look of hope to my mum's face.

Well everywhere we drove we saw little groups of people out and about hunting or pretending to hunt around the trees. I saw some of the line-dancers had a banner saying *Pobby and Dingan Search Party*. One big black bloke was standing on a mullock heap looking through a pair of binoculars. I recognised he was the man who brought Kellyanne home one time when his son kicked her in the shin and pulled her long hair when they were playing out behind the service station. Dad called him 'the good coon' because he was dead-crazy about opals, and one time I'd seen him doing a traditional mating dance at the wet T-shirt competition. When we drove up in the ute he came over and poked his head through the window on Kellyanne's side and did a big grin and said, 'Don' worry, girl. I'll find Pobby and Dingan in a flash for ya. I ain't Lightning Dreaming for nothing. I'm gonna go walkabout 'til I find them.' And then he walked off into the bush. After that I didn't see him again for weeks, but.

Well I think Kellyanne was pretty amazed by all this, because her eyes were wide open. She turned and whispered to me, 'Are all these people looking for Pobby and Dingan?'

'That's right,' I said. 'Even the abos.'

Kellyanne didn't say anything after that. We took her back home and she went to sleep a little more peacefully. But when Jack the Quack came around later in the evening my mum was in floods of tears. I knew then that he must have told her my little sis was really very ill and that my plan to make her feel better had failed. I went and hid in my room feeling like there was a rock in my throat.

My dad went walkabout that night. I heard him leaving. He was sniffing and sobbing and breathing heavy like a kettle.

SIX

I woke up in the middle of the night all restless. I got out of bed, pulled open my car door, and slid out of the room. A light was on in the living-room and my mum was sitting on the floor with her back towards me and her chin resting on her knee. I tiptoed up to her and saw she had something rectanglish in her hand. 'What you looking at, Mum?' I asked.

My mum almost blasted off like a rocket. She jumped up on to her feet and turned around to face me all in one move. She was holding her hands out in a weird kind of karate chop. But when she saw it was me she calmed down and stopped trembling. She said, 'Hey, Ashmol! It's you! Not sleepy?' I noticed she had put the thing she was holding behind her back.

'What were you looking at, Mum?' I said.

Colour went over her cheeks like rolling-flash. 'Oh. It's just a photograph, Ashmol.'

'Mind if I see? I really need something to knacker-out my eyes so as I can sleep.'

Mum paused for a while, and then handed me the

photograph with a trembling hand and sat back down on the floor. I sat down opposite her, cross-legged. The photograph was of four people standing in a line with their arms around each other. Two blokes and two women. Behind them was a sort of a hill with trees on it and the side of a building. And the hill was covered with purple dots. The sky was a mixture of blue patches and very bulging sorts of grey clouds. But the most amazing thing about the photo was the purple dots.

'What are those?' I asked, pointing at the dots.

'Bluebells,' said Mum. 'It's a photograph taken in England, Ashmol.'

'And who're those guys in the line?' I asked, scanning over their faces. The girls were very pretty and the blokes looked smart and rich and totally into-themselves. And the blokes had on expensive black suits and sharp noses, and the sheilas had flowers in their hair and pale skin and dresses like they wear at the Opal Princess competition.

'That's me, Ashmol,' said my mum, in a whisper. 'Aged nineteen. In Granny Pom's paddock before the Castleford Ball.'

'What?' I said. 'Which one?' And I looked again at the photo and saw her immediately. But she looked so different it was amazing. Much sparklier and cleaner in the photograph. Slimmer and with longer hair, but not as pretty as now, that's for sure. And then I noticed one of the blokes was holding his face next to my mum's, and was looking at her real close, and his hand was on her bare shoulder.

'Who's that bloke?'

'Which one?'

'That one.' I pointed to the man in the photograph with the side parting and the hand.

'Peter Sidebottom.'

'Peter what?'

'Peter Juvenal Whiteway Sidebottom.'

'That's a funny sort of a name,' I said. 'Was he a mate of yours?'

'Yes. He was.' My mum paused and did her long-look-out-of-the-window thing. 'He was my boyfriend before I met your father, as a matter of fact,' she said.

'Oh,' I said, a bit embarrassed and not sure what to say next. 'Did he know the Queen?'

My mum laughed. 'You're a funny boy, Ashmol! What do you mean: *Did he know the Queen?*'

'Well, he looks sort of rich,' I said, 'and like he might know that royal family and go shopping with them or something,' I said.

'No. He didn't know the Queen,' said my mum. 'But you're right, Ashmol. He was rich. Well, his parents were, anyway. Now he's left England and gone to live in a place called New York in America.'

I felt a bit hot under the hair and I sort of didn't want to be in the room any more. But my legs weren't going nowhere and my mouth was still wanting to talk.

'Mum, were you going to marry this Juvenile Sidebottom?' I asked.

My mum thought long and hard about this one and then said, 'Perhaps. But that was before your father swept me off my feet.' I felt sort of sick inside when I heard this.

'I bet that Juvenile Sidebottom's a total dag,' I said. 'And I bet he's not half as happy in New York as we are here at the Ridge.'

'Are you happy here at the Ridge, Ashmol?' my mum asked, not taking her eyes off herself and Peter Sidebottom in the photo.

'Sure as hell am,' I said, forcing out a big smile. 'And you want to know why? Because here there's always opal waiting to be found, and there's always something to dream about like another Fire Bird or a Christmas Beetle or a Southern Princess or an Aurora Australis.'

'Well, yes, I suppose that's true,' said my mum a little sadly.

'And I reckon my dad is going to find something real special pretty soon,' I went on, 'because he may not have been first in line when the money got handed out, and he may have rocks in his head, and he may have the rough end of the pineapple at the moment, but he's a pretty amazing sort of a dad all in all.' Well then I stood up and walked back towards the door, but before I went out I said, 'One thing's for sure, I'm bloody glad I ain't called Ashmol Juvenile Sidebottom!' Then I walked out of the living room and closed the door behind me, and I heard my mum call after me in a wobbly voice, 'Goodnight, Ashmol Williamson! See you in the morning, hey?'

SEVEN

The next day people came up to our camp saying they had
found Pobby and Dingan. When I made my plan I hadn't
reckoned people would actually claim they had found the
imaginary friends and come for their reward. The trouble
was I hadn't got a reward to reward them with because I
hadn't thought that far ahead. I always just sort of thought
Kellyanne would find them by herself when she realised
other people were taking an interest, like. But no. At
nine o'clock in the morning Fat Walt, who owned
the house-made-completely-from-bottles, came out and
knocked on the door calling out, 'Hey, little Kellyanne
Williamson! I got yer Pobby and Dingan right here wi'
me!' He strode in holding his arms outstretched like he
was carrying a bundle of dirty washing or something. I
looked at him with a doubtful expression, knowing it
wasn't going to work. 'Found them out at Coocoran, I
did,' he said proudly.

I led him through to Kellyanne's bedroom. I said,
'Kellyanne! Fat Walt's here! Says he's found Pobby and
Dingan.'

Kellyanne opened her eyes and I helped her sit up.

Fat Walt came through into the bedroom. 'Here they are, Kellyanne,' he said. 'They're asleep. I found them out at Coocoran. They was shooting roos and they must have dozed off under a tree.'

Kellyanne closed her eyes again and pulled up the covers. 'Stop pretending,' she said. 'You haven't got Pobby and Dingan there, anyone can see that. Pobby and Dingan don't sleep and they don't shoot. They're pacifists. You've got nothing in your arms but thin air, and you know it.'

Walt looked defeated. He said something like, 'Well, have it your way then, you little Williamson brat!' and walked out. I felt sort of sorry for him all in all.

An hour later the legendary Domingo from the castle came in all excited, mopping his forehead with a cloth. His hands were all blistered from all that lugging of rocks and castle-building he had been doing and he wore a pair of boots and blue socks pulled up to his knees. He yelled, 'Hey, you fellas! You'll never guess what I found roaming around the dungeon in my castle, all lost and bewildered? Yup – your friends Pobby and Dingan. They said they'd walked twenty miles back from some opal fields. Well, you can relax now, mate, because Domingo has found them and now I've come to claim my reward. They're back at the castle waiting to be collected.'

'What did Pobby and Dingan say when you found them?' asked Kellyanne in her weak little voice.

Domingo thought carefully and scratched at his chin, and said, 'Hmm, well, they said they were very relieved and they wanted to see their best friend Kellyanne Williamson and have a big meal of steak and chips because they were bloody starving.'

'No they didn't,' said Kellyanne. 'Pobby and Dingan only eat Cherry Ripes and Violet Crumbles and lollies.'

Domingo looked a mite desperate. 'Maybe they've outgrown them now,' he said. You had to give him points for quick thinking. But Kellyanne wasn't having any of it. She rolled over in her bed saying, 'I wish people would stop making up such stupid stories about finding Pobby and Dingan. This whole town is going crazy. They should go back to their mines. I need to get some more sleep.'

I led Domingo out saying I was real sorry, and thanks for trying at least, and he sloped off back to his half-built castle shrugging his shoulders and kicking at the dirt. 'Seems to me she doesn't want to find them at all,' he said. I was worried he was also thinking: I reckon Rex Williamson's a ratter. But anyway he shook my hand and went off to work on his turrets and to wait for his dream princess to arrive on her flying horse.

All in all about ten people in total came that day claiming they had found Pobby and Dingan. One old lady turned up with a little jar saying she had caught them in it. Ken from the chemist's came in all stooped over saying he was giving Dingan a piggyback. He made out he had found her with a broken leg. He said he hadn't found Pobby yet but would go back to the same place he found Dingan and have a scout around. Joe Lucas who won the log-throwing competition the year before reckoned he'd found Pobby and Dingan drunk in his grandpa's wine cellar. He spent about twenty minutes doing this conversation thing in front of Kellyanne to try and make her laugh. He pretended to be trying to keep Pobby and Dingan under control and cracked lots of good jokes. A girl called Venus turned up with her Alsatian saying her dog had sniffed out the imaginary friends. Even the little boy with the Eric the ninja platypus came along claiming that his own imaginary friend had found my sister's friends. He reckoned it was only possible for imaginary friends to be found by other imaginary friends. He did the best job of all of them. But at the end of the day Eric and him were sent away with their tails between their legs. Kellyanne said that there was no way Pobby and Dingan would come back with a giant ninja platypus because giant ninja platypuses don't exist. Anyone knows that.

EIGHT

Well, for a day or so all this action perked up Kellyanne a bit. It perked Lightning Ridge up too, I reckon. People around here like to get ahold of weird things, and they got so involved with the idea of Pobby and Dingan and my sister Kellyanne that they seemed to forget about Dad and Old Sid the Grouch for a while. And no one had tried to burn down our fence recently either. But even though everyone was giving her plenty of attention, Kellyanne still wasn't eating. She really did think that Pobby and Dingan had died now, and all she could talk about was bringing their corpses back. She said she'd feel plenty better if she could just be with their dead bodies. But bodies still need finding. I was getting a bit impatient with all this and so I said, 'Kellyanne, you're worrying Mum and Dad sick. Everyone's trying to help, but you know damn well that you're the only one that's ever going to find Pobby and Dingan or Pobby and Dingan's bodies or whatever. Now either find them or forget about them so you can get better and we can go back to normal!'

Kellyanne looked like she was thinking this one over

and over. Eventually my sister said, 'Ashmol. Please can you go out one more time to Wyoming and go down the mine. I've got a hunch about it. A sort of a feeling.'

'What? You want me to go down the mine looking for Pobby and Dingan?'

'Please. And go alone and at night so that people won't be able to see you, and you won't get into trouble.'

'You think they'll be there?'

'Like I said. I've got a hunch.' She put her head on the pillow and pulled the blanket up to her chin. 'Maybe they got lost in the drives and their bodies are still lying there in the dark all starved.'

'Supposing I go,' I said. 'How will I know it's them? I can't *see* Pobby and Dingan like you can. Never could.'

Kellyanne didn't answer. She had fallen asleep, and her arm was thin and deathly-looking. There were rings under her eyes and her face was the colour of shin-cracker.

NINE

So that night I got dressed into warm clothes and took a sausage from the fridge and put it in my pocket. I could hear Mum and Dad talking in their room in murmurs. I also got a ball of string out of the garage. I crept out of our camp and tiptoed over to where I keep my bike lying down in the dirt. I pushed it out of the drive so it didn't clank too much. And then I tied my little pocket torch to the handlebars with a bootlace and started the long journey out to the Wyoming claim. My heart was beating so hard it was like someone was pedalling inside of me.

When I was half the way out to Wyoming I stopped and asked myself what the hell I was doing going looking in the middle of the night for two dead people who didn't exist. It seemed like a pretty stupid thing for a kid to be doing. I almost made up my mind to turn around and go back, pretending I'd found the corpses of Pobby and Dingan straight away. But I knew Kellyanne wouldn't believe me. So I decided just to go and have a look down the mine shaft, and hang out there for an hour or so, so that at least I could say I'd been down and done my best. I thought Kellyanne would appreciate that. And she'd think I'd come a long way since the days when I used to punch the air where Pobby and Dingan were supposed to be. And I didn't want her to die thinking I was the kind of Ashmol who didn't believe anything.

Well, it was a good ten miles of cold road to the claim and once I got off on to the dirt tracks it became harder to see where the hell I was going. I had to weave my way in and out of the burs and bindies. Luckily I sort of knew the way across the wheat paddock to the Wyoming claim blindfolded because I'd been out there so many times with Dad. But I still had to guide my bike along the tracks without going down any potholes or knocking into any rocks. It was scary, though, being out there on my own, and so to brave me up a bit I kept pretending to be James Blond and I made myself a Colt 45 revolver out of two fingers and a cocked-back thumb and held it down by the leg of my trousers as I rode along. I swear for about fifteen minutes I almost forgot I was Ashmol Williamson altogether.

Well, it was now so quiet that I could hear the blood in my head creeping around and my teeth chattering together. Plus there was this huge sky with stars peppered all over it, and I remembered Dad telling me that for each star in the sky there was an opal in the earth, and that opals are hidden from view because they are even prettier than stars and the sight of a whole lot of them would break people's hearts. And I also remembered him telling me that all this land where Lightning Ridge is now was once covered by sea-water and how all kinds of sea creatures had been found fossilised in the rock. I felt a shiver go down my spine just thinking about how strange this was that a sea was once here where now there is nothing but dry land. And suddenly I thought how maybe if this amazing thing was true it was just possible Pobby and Dingan were true too. But then I told myself, 'Jesus, mate, you're losing your marbles, you fruit-loop. Snap out of it.' And that made me bike a little faster towards my dad's opal claim.

When I got there I undid my torch and turned it off. I laid down my Chopper and tiptoed off carefully because I was worried that Old Sid might wake up and think I was ratting his claim. See, ever since my dad punched him in the face for calling him a ratter everyone knew that Sid stayed up late with a candle burning in his caravan, eating his frill-neck lizards and holding a gun out of his window. And I also knew he had bought a guard dog which was why I put a sausage in my pocket.

Sure enough Sid's dog ran out barking. He was attached to Sid's caravan by a rope. I threw him the sausage and crept over to our mine, taking care not to trip on the starpicket or fall down any holes that had been left uncovered. I heard that dog slobbering in the dark. When I got to the mine shaft I remembered how my dad would always say, 'Always put your lid on when you go underground, kiddo!' – and so I tiptoed over to our old caravan and took out a yellow mining helmet from underneath it. I put on the hat and tightened the strap up under my chin. And that made me feel a little better. Then I tied my torch to my belt by the bootlace.

The mine shaft was narrow and dark. I lowered myself down carefully on to the ladder. There was only enough room on each rung for my toes and so I had to grip extra hard on to the sides with my hands as I climbed down in case I lost my footing. Normally my dad came down with a cord and a lightbulb thing that's attached to the generator, but all I had was my little one-battery torch which didn't let off too much light.

One foot after the other I went down backwards, trying not to think about how I would end up if I fell. After every five steps I took a breather to make sure I was still alive and on the ladder and not at the bottom in a heap. And the further I went down the more I felt like I was in some throat, being swallowed by some monster.

Well, pretty soon my foot was on the bottom rung and I was standing on the floor of the ballroom. It felt like I was still on the ladder because I could feel where the rungs had been pressing into my feet.

Before I set off into the darkness I remembered the story Kellyanne had told me from her *Book of Heroes and Legends* about a Greek bloke who went into an opal mine to kill a giant huntsman spider, and how he took a ball of wool so he could follow it back out and not get lost in the drives. And that's why I'd packed a ball of string. I tied it to the bottom rung of the ladder and went off down the drive. I was concentrating so damn hard on what I was doing that I nearly forgot why I had come in the first place.

I set off across the ballroom, flashing my torch around and being careful not to walk into any props. The light of my torch lit up the red clay. I kept thinking I could see weird, wrinkly faces looking at me from the walls. And as I went further the faces became faces of people I knew or had heard something about. And one of those faces was like Old Sid's and one was Jack the Quack and one was the bloke with the stinking breath who almost clobbered me at the Digger's Rest. And one was Peter Juvenile Sidebottom. I put my mind off all these faces by saying out loud, 'Sandstone and clay. Sandstone and clay. Sandstone and clay,' over and over again just to remind myself what a load of hooey all this face stuff was.

I took the drive on the left, ducking my head the whole time, even though I didn't need to by a long shot. I kept walking, unravelling the string as I went and keeping an ear out for the slide of a snake.

Well, I knew these drives pretty well, but after a bit I found a new tunnel on my left which I hadn't ever been in before. There was a strange monkey in the left wall.

And a monkey isn't a thing that swings through the trees but the word we miners use for a sort of a hole. And I figured it must be where Dad had been jackhammering recently because he had left his pick there. Well, there was a smell of some kind which I'd never smelt here before. I reckoned it might just be the smell you get at night down an opal drive because I'd never been out in one at night like this. Anyway, I went through the monkey and as far as I could go along the new drive.

Well, right in this corner I waved the torch around until I suddenly saw something pretty unusual. There was a massive heap of rubble in the corner. It wasn't just opal dirt and tailings. Oh no, it seemed like the whole part of the roof had collapsed and fallen in like a big mushroom. The first thing I thought was: Shit, that means some more of the roof might fall down on top of me. I turned to follow my string back to the ladder, thinking that the last thing my family needed right now was a squashed Ashmol, when suddenly I had this peculiar kind of mind-flash which made me freeze in my tracks. I said to myself, 'What if Pobby and Dingan got caught under the pile of rock?' And then I listened carefully and sort of convinced myself that I could hear a little moaning and breathing. And then I, Ashmol Williamson, found myself calling their names. I really did. 'Pobby! Dingan! Don't worry, Ashmol is here! Kellyanne's brother! Pobby and Dingan! I'm here to rescue you.' But then I remembered that Kellyanne was convinced they were dead, and that meant they probably were. And so I took off the stones more slowly and didn't hurry so much. But I was so excited I could have filled up a bucket with my sweat and sent it up on the hoist.

I set about on hands and knees taking off rocks and moving them to one side until I got to the floor. And there suddenly, right in front of me was the wrapper of a Violet Crumble chocolate bar. And it was just great to see something a little familiar with those good old words written on it way out here in the middle of nowhere. But then suddenly my eye caught hold of something else flashing up at me. Something sitting there in the dark. Waiting. A sort of greeny-red glint. I headed straight for it. It was a nobbie the size of a yo-yo, and when I shone my torch on it I could see there was a bit of colour there. My heart beat the world record for the pole vault. I brushed the dirt off as best I could and then I licked the nobbie. It was opal. Green. Red. Black. All of them together. It was strangely warm like it had already been in someone's hand or close to someone's skin. I sat there for a while, my heart doing a back-flip, thinking: Shit, we Williamsons are going to be rich bastards! I rolled it around in my palm and licked the dirt off again to make it shine. And I reckoned the opalised bit was as bright as a star and the size of a coin, or a bellybutton. And that gave me the idea. This was Dingan's bellybutton. This was Pobby and Dingan who got trapped under the roof of the drive where it fell in. And the smell I smelt earlier was death. And the last thing they ate before they died was a Violet Crumble. Everything sort of fat together perfectly.

I put the nobbie in my shoe and the Violet Crumble wrapper in my pocket, and my torch in my mouth and took up the bodies of Pobby and Dingan in my arms. They were heavier than I'd thought. Much, much heavier. I made my way back along the drive towards the foot of the ladder, the torch moving along the browny-red walls. And I found myself groaning and muttering as I dragged Pobby and Dingan back. There was something heavy about the air too, if you know what I mean.

At the foot of the ladder I paused and set Pobby and Dingan down gently, remembering that there was no way a little bloke like me was going to get them up to the top all by myself. So I laid them both down and took off my coat and draped it over them. As I climbed up the ladder I kept looking back down over my shoulder to make sure the corpses were still at the bottom. And then I got back on my Chopper and pedalled back home under a sky which was still laid up with opal-fever. I was colder than any cold thing a bloke could think of.

TEN

I didn't sleep the rest of that long night, but when the morning finally showed up I walked into Kellyanne's room to tell her what had happened. Everything smelt a bit of sick. I shook Kellyanne on the shoulder and said, 'Wake up, Sis. I've got to show you something. Wake up!' Kellyanne's eyelids fluttered and her eye peeped out. She looked like she didn't have much life left in her. I felt sort of desperate. It was going to be me against death. Me on my own. Not James Blond not Luke Skywalker or nobody, but just Ashmol Williamson speaking to save his sister's life. I'd seen Fat Walt and the legendary Domingo and Joe Lucas and all those others fail. I kind of knew this was my last chance and so I took a real deep breath.

'I did what you said, Kellyanne – I went down the mine last night – and guess what – the roof had collapsed in one of the drives – Pobby and Dingan got caught under it – I know it because I found the opal that Dingan wore in her bellybutton – they were lying all bruised in the mine – they were – honest – they were there – and they were dead. But they looked peaceful, like – they were lying together holding hands – and they was still a little warm and everything.'

Tears started coming out of my eyes, maybe cos I was knackered, but also because I was damn worried that Kellyanne wasn't going to believe a word of what I was saying. I was afraid that if I stopped talking she would suddenly turn and say, 'Stop being a drongo, Ashmol. That wasn't Pobby and Dingan,' so I just sort of spouted everything out in a big blabber. 'They had their eyes closed, Kellyanne – in Pobby's hand was a Violet Crumble wrapper.' I waved the wrapper around while I was talking to try and get her attention. 'You can see for youself, Sis – I left the bodies laid out at the claim under my coat – because I couldn't lift them – see – and if you come with me I'll show you – but you gotta believe me – they were there – I lifted off the rocks and I could smell them – really – the roof came down on top of them – there were no props or pillars – it came down and squashed them – honest – I dragged them back to the ladder – but I couldn't get 'em up – I really couldn't.'

Well then I looked at the floor and sort of rubbed my ankles together, and cracked the joints in my fingers.

'Can I see the opal?' Kellyanne whispered after a while.

I took off my shoe and held out the opal in the palm of my hand which was shaking like a fish. I suddenly got really worried because I thought: This opal doesn't look like nothing anyone would put in their bellybutton. It was too big.

But Kellyanne sat up suddenly and put her arms around my neck and said, 'Ashmol! You've found the bodies.

You've found Pobby and Dingan! This is it! This is the stone that Dingan wears in her bellybutton!'

When I heard this I was suddenly all unplugged and relieved and excited. This huge smile had taken hold of Kellyanne's face. It was like a big rock had been lifted off her. I suddenly thought: Great! It's all over! I've done it! Now Kellyanne will get better and everything's going to be fine.

But Kellyanne looked at me and said, 'Now all you've got to do, Ashmol, is arrange the funeral.'

'What?' I thought for a minute she was talking about her own funeral.

'All people have funerals. And so must Pobby and Dingan. I can't relax until they're buried, Ashmol. I'd do it myself, but I can't because I have to go to the hospital in Walgett for a few days.'

She looked at me again with those tired eyes. I wasn't too sure the hospital would be able to get rid of the dark rings around them.

'You can pay for it with the bellybutton,' she said. 'That's what Dingan would have wanted. That's what she always said. "When I die," she said, "pay for my funeral with my bellybutton stone."'

'How much does a funeral cost?'

'A fortune, I think,' Kellyanne replied. 'But the opal should just about cover it.'

My heart sank when I heard this. I never knew death was so expensive. I had reckoned on buying a new house and getting my mum an air ticket for a holiday in England, and all kinds of other stuff with the money from that opal. But I made up my mind there and then that the most important thing was getting Kellyanne well again, and that if that meant trading an amazing opal for a grave for Pobby and Dingan, then that was what I was going to do.

'I'll only do it if you get better and stop worrying the hell out of Mum and Dad,' I said all firm. 'And only if you promise not to go dying because then I'll have another funeral to arrange and that's going to be a real chore.'

'I promise,' said Kellyanne. 'Thanks, Ashmol. And now you promise me something too. Promise you won't tell Mum and Dad about finding Dingan's opal.'

'OK. OK.'

'And that you won't go showing it to anyone except the funeral director.'

'I promise.'

'And don't go trying to get any money for it. This isn't your opal, and it's not Dad's opal either, Ashmol. This is Dingan's bellybutton. It isn't some ordinary stone you can go making a heap of money from.'

I thought about this long and hard, and I thought what a shame it was that I was going to be giving away my first red on black. And then I said:

'I promise not to go making any money on it.' And then I left the room, almost worn out with promising.

ELEVEN

So the next day, after Mum and Dad had gone off with
Kellyanne to take her to the hospital, I walked out on
the road that goes past the golf course and out to the
cemetery. I walked past the sign which says *Lightning Ridge
Population – ?* And the question mark is there cos of all the
people who pass through, find nothing and give up and go
back home. And because of all the folks out hidden at their
mines in the bush. And all the criminals and that who don't
care to register themselves on the electoral roll. My mum
said she reckoned there were around eight thousand and
fifty-three plus Pobby and Dingan, that's eight thousand
and fifty-five residents out at the Ridge altogether. But
now Pobby and Dingan were dead I guess it was back to
eight thousand and fifty-three.

As I walked I turned Dingan's bellybutton around in
my fingers. I had been so busy I hadn't had a hell of a lot
of time to look at it. It was pretty incredible. A mixture
of black and greens, and when you turned it a flash of red
went shivering through it from side to side. And it was
wrapped up cosy in a doona of white and brown rock. It

had good luck written all over it, that's for sure. And it was warm from the Lightning Ridge sun.

I finally got to the cemetery and I had a good look around. I'd never been there before. It's a small quiet place not far at all from some mines and about the size of two claims strung together. If you look hard you can see the tops of drilling rigs peeking over the trees like dinosaurs or skeletons of giraffes. Well, you could tell which ones of the dead people had struck opal and which hadn't because some of the signs were cut out of stone and marble, and some were just two bits of rotting wood crossed over. Kellyanne was right. Death looked like it was just too expensive for some people. Plus it was weird thinking of all those dead people under the ground, especially when you thought about how a lot of the dead folks had spent their lives working under the ground as well. Many of the signs said *Killed in Mining Accident*. And there were flowers and colourful stones under their names and most of them said R.I.P. I used to think that meant they'd sort of been ripped out of their lives like opal ripped out of the clay.

I noticed that Bob the Swede had a bit of space next to his grave. Room enough for two more I thought, if old Bobby-boy budged over a bit. There was graves for little kids who died young as well. They were under piles of earth like the mullock heaps out at the mines, only reddy-brown. I suddenly felt mighty sad about Kellyanne and I was thinking what it might be like if she had to be buried out here in a sad little grave with a few plastic flowers in front, and all because of a couple of imaginary friends who died out in my dad's mine. But I told myself to stop thinking like this, and that everything was going to be OK now because I'd managed by some fluke to find the bodies. She'd get better once she'd mourned at the funeral I was going to buy with Dingan's bellybutton stone. There were tears in my eyes, but. Maybe it was cos I had to get rid of my first opal. Anyway, I think it was only the second time I ever had them in my whole life.

TWELVE

I knocked on the door of Mr Dan Dunkley the funeral director. A voice said, 'Come in.' I turned the handle of his door and entered.

Mr Dan was a fat man with too many chins for his own good. His office was spick and span – well, spick, anyway – and he was sitting at his desk with his cheek in his flabby white hand. Behind him he had a grinding wheel going and a couple of dibbers and dob-sticks laid out on a tray next to a bottle of methylated spirits and a Little Dixie Combination Assembly. On his forehead Mr Dan had his weird glasses for looking at opals. Like most people out at the Ridge who don't have the guts to mine, he did a bit of cutting and buying and selling on the side to keep him ticking over when not enough people were kicking the bucket.

Mr Dan looked up at me. He didn't know who I was, unlike most people, and my guess is he wasn't too sociable and only got to know people when they had croaked it. I said, 'My name is Ashmol Williamson and I have come to talk graves.'

Mr Dan took off his specs and did a frown and lit up his pipe. After a while he muttered, 'School project?'

'No sir,' I said. 'You may have heard about my sister Kellyanne Williamson? She's dying.'

Well I figured he was bound to twig when I told him Kellyanne's name. He probably had her coffin all ready and made-up out back. Sure enough a bit of a nod came up on his face.

'Reason she's dying is she lost two of her friends a while back. And she's sad,' I said.

'Oh,' said Mr Dan. 'I didn't know that. All I know about you Williamsons is that your daddy's in a spot of trouble.'

I walked over and bunked myself up on to Mr Dunkley's desk and sat there like a cat looking at him. 'These friends of my sister,' I said, 'they went missing. They were gone a few days and nobody could find them.'

Mr Dan suddenly looked interested. 'I didn't know any of this.'

'Well. You're the only one who doesn't,' I said. 'See, that's the reason you ain't had too many people coming in with opals to sell recently. Everybody's been out looking for Pobby and Dingan all day long. Nobody's been mining.'

'Are you sure you ain't making this up, kid?'

'Positive,' I said, all confident and smart like James Blond.

Mr Dan walked over and switched the grinding wheel off.

'Well, boy, what do you want me to do? Go looking for two kids down a hole? Happens all the time, little fella. Kids don't take any notice of where they're going cos they got their heads in the clouds, and then they trip up and fall. Wham! Splat!' Mr Dan whopped his hand down hard on his desk.

There was a silence, and then I looked at him and said, 'There's no point in going looking for them, Mr Dan. I don't want you to do that. The thing is these two friends of my sister's, they are sort of imaginary. They don't exist. They's invisible. And besides, I've found them, or found their bodies any rate. They're dead.'

Mr Dan almost choked on his pipe. He sighed and said, 'Listen, kid. Ashley, or whatever you're called, I'm a busy bloke. Now hop it.'

'I noticed there is a space next to Bob the Swede in the cemetery,' I said, refusing to budge.

Mr Dan took the glasses off his forehead. 'You been playin' around in my cemetery, kid?'

I didn't see how he could claim it was his cemetery. The dead owned it. It was their claim. Or else they were ratting it under his nose.

'I wanna buy that space for a grave for Pobby and Dingan,' I told Mr Dan. 'You see, I don't think my sis is going to get better until she sees them buried once and for all.'

'You can't bury imaginary people,' said Mr Dan. 'There's nothing to bury.'

'Believe what you want, Mr Dan,' I answered. 'Just let me buy the claim. Let me have a space in the cemetery.'

'What you offering?'

'Opal.'

I took off my right shoe and fished out Dingan's bellybutton. I had chipped off all the dirt and polished it up with a cloth so it looked better than ever. So beautiful and sparkling. My fingers didn't like handing it over. Mr Dan Dunkley took it in his big hand and held it under his light. I was all twitchy and I never took my eyes off it once.

'Fuck me dead!' he said. 'Where d'you get this, kid? You rat this? You better not have ratted this. Where d'you get it?' I never saw anyone put on his opal-glasses so quick.

'Noodling.'

'You found this noodling?'

'Yup. Noodling on a mullock heap at my dad's claim.'

'This don't look like no opal some kid found noodling on his dad's mullock heap. I reckon you ratted it from Old Sid.'

I started getting a bit pissed at this. I suppose I was beginning to feel like Kellyanne and Dad. It wasn't too cool having folks not believing what you were saying all the time.

'I bloody well did not,' I said.

'This is a valuable stone. This is worth a lot of money, kid,' said Mr Dan.

'Is it worth as much as a grave and a couple of coffins?' I asked him.

Mr Dan sharpened up his eyes and looked me up and down. He leant closer over his desk.

'Just about,' he said in a whisper. 'Your daddy know about this, son?'

'Nope. And I don't want him to. Because if he knew about it, Mr Dan, then he'd go crazy with excitement and then he wouldn't let me buy Pobby and Dingan a grave with it, and then Kellyanne wouldn't get any better.'

'Anybody else know?'

'Nobody 'cept Kellyanne.'

Dan Dunkley held the stone under the light again and twisted it around so the red flash streaked across it. I could see those colours coming up beautiful and I knew I was on to a winner.

'OK, son. You got a deal,' said Mr Dan. 'I'll let you have the grave for the opal.'

'Great!' I said. 'And I want you to arrange the funeral for Pobby and Dingan too, Mr Dan,' I said. 'And make it realistic. My sis won't get better if it's not realistic. You better make it like a funeral for two normal kids and make them coffins and everything and read some Bible stuff. Make it on Sunday at eleven.'

'I'll talk to the preacher,' said Mr Dan, not taking his eyes off Dingan's bellybutton stone. 'And you'd better talk to him too. He's gonna think I'm doolally or something.'

THIRTEEN

I walked out of Dan Dunkley's house a little dazed. I was pleased I'd got a space for Pobby and Dingan in the cemetery, but I had a hollow, aching feeling behind my ribs which wouldn't go away. I couldn't believe an opal had passed through my hands so quick. An opal I had found on my lonesome on the Williamsons' claim at Wyoming. I felt like I was living in a dream or something. Everything was moving so fast.

The preacher was a small weedy man drinking beer from a green bottle on the stump of a sandalwood tree around the back of his pokey white church. I told him what was what. After a long pause he looked at me and said, 'OK, I'll do it, young Ashmol. Now you'd better give me some hard facts about these little imaginary friends so I can make me a speech.'

I thought about it long and hard. Eventually I said, 'Well, vicar, they was quiet and they always went around together. And they liked chewing lollies, and Violet Crumbles and Cherry Ripes.'

The preacher noted these things down on his

pad. He repeated the words 'Violet Crumbles' and 'Cherry Ripes'.

'And they used to go and bathe at the Bore Baths with Kellyanne.'

And then I reeled off a sort of list of all the things I had learnt about Pobby and Dingan:

Pobby was a boy and the oldest by a year.

Dingan was the pretty one. Real pretty. And smart as a fox.

They didn't leave no footprints because they walked in the same place as Kellyanne.

And Pobby and Dingan weren't scared of the big kids in Lightning Ridge.

And Dingan read books over your shoulder.

And Pobby liked going out to dance in the lightning storms.

And Dingan could run real quick and play rigaragaroo.

And they liked Kellyanne better than anyone else.

And Pobby had a kind of limp, and when Kellyanne was late for anything she always said Pobby slowed her up and she was late because she had to wait for him.

And Pobby could walk through walls.

The preacher made some more jottings and I saw him running out of page.

And Dingan had an opal in her bellybutton.

And Kellyanne always sat in between Pobby and Dingan on the bus to Walgett.

And Dingan was a pacifist because every time I stamped on her or punched her air and said, 'If Dingan is real why doesn't she hit back?' Kellyanne would say, 'Cos Dingan is a pacifist, stupid.'

And they was generous, because Kellyanne was always thanking them for being nice to her.

And they talked English or whistled to make themselves understood.

And you had to be a certain kind of person to hear them.

The preacher had stopped writing and was staring into space. 'Thanks, Ashmol,' he said. 'That's plenty of information. Now take care of your sister and I'll see you on Sunday.'

'Will Pobby and Dingan go to heaven or hell, vicar?' I asked before I went. I was sort of testing him out to see if he'd take Kellyanne's friends seriously.

The preacher thought long and hard about this and said, 'What do *you* think?'

'Heaven,' I said firmly, 'so long as there's Violet Crumbles there.'

'I think you're right,' said the preacher and took another swig out of his green bottle. As I rode off on my

Chopper he shouted, 'I shall be praying for your father, Ashmol Williamson!'

'Do what you want, vicar!' I called back. 'Just come up with the goods.'

I zoomed off down the road thinking about heaven. It was like the ballroom of an opal mine. Full of people with lamps on their heads. And everyone was singing Elvis Presley songs and gouging, and swinging picks.

FOURTEEN

Before I got home I stopped off at Humph's Moozeum, which is a place full of amazing junk. The Moozeum is just down from the half-built castle which the bloke Domingo who I told you about was building single-handed out there in the middle of nowhere. That's Lightning Ridge for you. People go all weird on you all the time because it's so hot and they start building castles and shit.

The man who owns the Moozeum is called Humph and he has spent his whole life collecting weird things. Well I liked to stop by and talk to him sometimes, and when I was sad it was a good place to go to cheer yourself up and get your mind on something else. There is a whole load of outhouses and old buses and cars and bits of mining machinery, and bush fridges, and there is a whole assortment of objects, old pictures, bones, bottles, books, sewing machines. There's a car up a tree and Humph even has the toes of one of his miner-friends pickled in a jar. He is getting some bloke's leg pickled too. He has a chunk of fossilised Turkish Delight from Gallipoli, and a bottle of vodka which he says a band called the Rolling Stones gave him. He is a clever old bugger, Humph. You never know if what he is saying is true.

One of the sections of the Moozeum is underground, and that's where I found old Humph sitting at the little bar he has in the corner. He was wearing a big floppy hat. 'Ah, Ashmol,' he said. 'Any news of Pobby and Dingan yet? Bit like looking for a needle in a haystack, I reckon.'

'Yeah, I found them,' I told him proudly. 'They were both dead.'

Old Humph didn't know whether to say 'Good' or 'That's too bad' and so he just grunted and held up something to show me. I trundled over and stood looking. I was pretty impressed. It was a framed invitation to the funeral of Princess Diana. And the writing was done in really fancy silver lettering and there was a royal stamp on it and everything. 'You got invited to the funeral of Princess Diana?' I asked with my eyes wide open.

'Did I hell!' said Humph, fairly splitting his sides with laughter. 'This little bewdy I cut out of a magazine and stuck down on a piece of card! Don't tell anyone, mind. The tourists love it.' That was Humph. He was a cunning old-timer who didn't care too much about the truth of things so long as there was a good story in it, and most of the time he told people about his fakes anyway so they could see how clever he'd been.

'Could you do me some invitations for Pobby and Dingan's funeral?' I asked.

'Having a funeral, are you?'

I nodded. 'I reckon Kellyanne won't get better until we bury the dead bodies and show them some last respect.'

Humph nodded solemnly. 'I wouldn't have minded having their dead bodies in my Moozeum,' he said. 'I haven't got any dead imaginary friends in my Moozeum yet. 'Bout the only thing I haven't got.'

'Maybe Kellyanne will let you get Pobby's finger pickled and put in a jar,' I suggested.

'Maybe,' said Humph, taking a swig of Johnnie Walker. 'So how many invitations do you want?'

'I want to invite everyone in Lightning Ridge.'

Humph nodded solemnly and scratched the top of his floppy hat.

'That makes eight thousand and fifty-three by my calculation,' I said.

FIFTEEN

The day of Dad's trial arrived. I wasn't allowed to go to the magistrates' court so I can't say exactly what happened. I can only imagine it. But the fat and the thin of it was that after he'd finished punishing someone for breaking and entering and when he had fined John the Gun and some other blokes for shooting too many roos, Judge McNulty made Dad stand up and tell the little jury about what he was doing out at Old Sid's mine that evening.

Well, this time my Dad didn't make up a lost cat story or make out he was just looking for his contact lenses. No way. He stood up straight and told them that he was out looking for Pobby and Dingan, the imaginary friends of his daughter Kellyanne Williamson, and that he was just checking to see if they'd wandered over on to Old Sid's claim. And Mum said that Judge McNulty looked all confused like a jigsaw puzzle before you put it together, and that he asked Dad to describe their appearance. I flinched a bit as I imagined my old man stuttering and tongue-twistering as he tried to get to grips with that one. Well my Dad must have handled it pretty well, but, because then McNulty moved straight on and asked whether Dad was on any drugs, and whether Dad thought the imaginary friends really existed. And apparently Dad looked old McNulty and the jury and everybody dead straight with his opal eyes and said that at first he thought they didn't exist, and then he wasn't too sure about it, and now he was positive they did exist after all because he was on trial for ratting because of them and he was a little angry with them for it too.

Judge McNulty rubbed his chin and scratched his head a lot. And then Old Sid, that whiskery bastard – as Mum called him – got up with a bandage over his nose and testified and called my father 'mentally deranged' and lots of other things including a 'low-down piece of roo shit'. And some of Old Sid's miner mates backed him up and talked a lot about how much my dad would drink and how he was always interested in other people's opal and where they had found it. And that confirmed he was a ratter as far as they could see. And then a policeman said how he saw Dad snotting Sid in the nose, only he didn't say snotting.

Well, according to Mum, the judge fidgeted around and whispered things to people. And then McNulty looked at the little jury and told them that the whole question of Mr Rex Williamson's guilt depended on whether it should be considered a crime to hit someone on the nose when they have called you a ratter and also on whether the jury believed he was really out looking for his daughter's imaginary friends that night. And he told the jury that meant they needed to work out for themselves how real they thought Pobby and Dingan were.

And Mum said you could see the jury mulling it over, and whispering the names Pobby and Dingan over plenty and she reckoned that most of them were thinking: Since half the town has been out looking for Pobby and Dingan, why couldn't it just be possible that the father of Kellyanne Williamson was looking as well? And then the jury heard from my dad that a funeral of Pobby and Dingan was taking place the next day, organised by his son Ashmol Williamson and if the judge wanted he and the jury could come along and see what real people they had been. And then Old Sid and his lawyer complained that the funeral had been dreamt up to distract from Rex Williamson's crime and that Pobby and Dingan were just invented on the spot as a sort of cover-up.

Mum told me that then Judge McNulty did lots of racking of his brains, and sometimes he looked a bit pale, but eventually he decided to break up the court until it was possible to interview Kellyanne. But he only did it after asking Sid about his family. And Sid said he hadn't got any, and that his wife had died twenty years ago. And the judge asked him if he ever talked to her privately even though she was dead. And Sid said he did sometimes when he was up at the agitator because his wife used to help him sift through opal dirt because she had better eyes than he did. But I don't think Sid realised what was going on, that the sly old Judge McNulty had trapped him into admitting that everybody has an imaginary friend of some kind even if you don't think they have, and that Old Sid himself was a bit on the short-sighted side.

After that, McNulty announced that the court was going to come together again when Kellyanne was better. And at the end of the proceedings only about twenty or thirty people were outside the courtroom to throw cabbages and things at my dad and hiss, 'Ratter. Ratter. Ratter. Ratter.' And only one bloke had a banner saying: POBBY AND DINGAN WERE RATTERS on it in red paint like blood.

SIXTEEN

Well, to be honest all this trial stuff cheered me up no end, and the next day Mum and me got ready for the funeral of Pobby and Dingan with smiles on our faces while Dad went off to fetch Kellyanne from the hospital.

Mum had bought me some new black pants and a black sweatshirt, and so we went out all comfortably to the cemetery and decorated the fence with flowers and opened up the gate. And the priest came and talked things through with us, you know, about what the proceedings were. And Mr Dan drove up around ten o'clock and shuffled around a little awkward in his suit and tie. And then the coffins of Pobby and Dingan turned up and I helped carry them up to the grave. And old Humph came along in his hat to tell me he was putting a plaque for Pobby and Dingan up in his Moozeum. Well, I was looking forward to telling Kellyanne this when she arrived from the hospital with Dad. That would put a massive smile on her face, for sure. And she would never be sick again.

And then all that was left to do was to wait for people to start arriving. I had some butterflies in my stomach, but. You see, I'd been round the whole of Lightning Ridge posting Humph's invitations into everybody's mail boxes. And I was sort of nervous to see how many came and how many tore up the invitations and still called us Williamsons a bunch of frigging lunatics. And I was also nervous because of the reports about Kellyanne and how she was getting worse by the day even though they'd managed to pump some food into her at the hospital. So it seemed pretty much like it was now or never.

I got so afraid that people wouldn't turn up and that I might have to imagine myself a whole crowd that I got really impatient and an hour before the funeral was due to start I got on my bike again and went pedalling around Lightning Ridge to see if people were getting ready. The place was a sort of deathly quiet. I sat on the step outside The Digger's Rest for half an hour trembling and half wanting to go for a piss.

Eventually a few people started stepping out of houses and shops coughing, or pulling back curtains and doors. And then suddenly as the sun got hotter in the sky, old buggers, young buggers, men and women and dogs started appearing on the street and walking out towards the cemetery. A couple of them saw me and waved. I got on my Chopper fast and cycled around the back way, standing up on the pedals to get a good view of the crowd walking along in silence between the gum trees and houses. And I noticed that everyone had, like, made an effort and changed out of their mining clothes into their best boardies and singlets.

I got back to the cemetery ahead of the people and I saw them all coming up the road past the balding little golf course like a massive great wave. I stood on Bob the Swede's gravestone and saw that actually there were many more than I'd expected. Thousands of people all coming out towards us. More even than you saw at the goat races, more even than I'd ever seen in my whole life except on the football on TV. And for a moment I was worried that there was something else going on that they were all going to, and that they were going to walk straight past the cemetery gates or something and head out of town.

But I shouldn't have worried because pretty soon the little cemetery was full of living people, and everyone closed in around the grave and the coffins which had Pobby and Dingan inside. Some sat on the scorched grass, and some wandered around looking at some of the other graves. And no one was saying nothing except a few words to each other. But most just gave me a nod and gazed out over the land or fanned themselves down. And Mum and me had made some lemonade and cookies earlier and so we passed some cups around and began pouring so that people had something to graze on. But although I was relieved to see all these people turn up at the cemetery for the funeral of Pobby and Dingan, the most important ones hadn't arrived. And that was Kellyanne and Dad.

Kellyanne and Dad. Dad and Kellyanne. They still hadn't come back from the hospital.

It was way past time for the funeral to start and people were starting to do a bit of muttering and all that. And I suppose some of them were starting to doubt if there was going to be a funeral at all. And perhaps some folks were beginning to look at each other and at me and my mum and starting to ask each other what the hell they were doing attending the funeral of two figments of a girl's imagination, especially when that little girl wasn't even there. And I remember picking out Judge McNulty in the crowd. He was frowning and looking at his watch. But at least the preacher was doing a good job. He was pretty sober and he was still going around welcoming people and saying hello and handing out sheets with some songs printed on them. I reckon he wasn't keen to lose all these people. Because if they stayed it would be the biggest congregation he ever preached to in his life. At one moment he looked up and gave me a thumbs-up sign as if to say, 'Don't worry, mate, Kellyanne will be here soon.'

And then suddenly she came. I recognised the sound of the ute as it came in the gate, and there was Dad at the wheel. And everyone turned around and stood watching as he climbed out and walked to the back and began to take out a fold-up wheelchair and assemble it on the grass. I ran down to meet him. Through the back window I could see Kellyanne's pale face. I ran to the back door and opened it and Kellyanne turned and gave me a twitch — because she had no strength for a whole smile. She was as thin as I have ever seen a person get, and Mum came and helped me lift her into the wheelchair which Dad had assembled. And there were tears in Mum's eyes and the funeral hadn't even started. Well then Mum gave Dad a big hug and a kiss right on the lips and I did a yuck sign to Kellyanne by sticking my finger down my throat, and then I pushed Kellyanne up the slope through the crowd and up to the grave of Pobby and Dingan. And most people I think were pretty shocked to see my sister looking so sick. And some of them said nice things to her on the way up like 'good on yer, gal' and 'she's a brave one'. And somebody else's mum put flowers on her lap. And then when she got to the top everyone suddenly started clapping and everyone was cheering and people were slapping my dad on the back. It took a fair while for everyone to settle down and listen to the preacher who was now standing up at the front and looking like he wanted to speak.

He shouted out, 'G-day, everybody! And welcome to the funeral of Pobby and Dingan, friends of Kellyanne Williamson and members of the good honest Williamson family!' Well at that point Humph let out a huge cheer, but he was the only one and I think he felt a bit of a drongo for doing it. But my dad had a little smile to himself. And then the preacher told us we were going to sing from our song sheets and everyone rustled their papers.

Well, Kellyanne had chosen the songs, and first we sang the Australian National Anthem. 'Australians all let us rejoice for we are young and free', and all that, and then Fingers Bill played a Cat Stevens song on his guitar and those who didn't know the words sort of just hummed it, and it went 'Oooh baby it's a wide world', or something like that. And Kellyanne had chosen it because it was Pobby and Dingan's favourite song. And it was quite amazing hearing all these people singing together. And I wouldn't say it was too tuneful or anything like that. But it was loud as hell and I reckon the emus out on the Moree Road didn't have no trouble hearing it.

Well then the preacher coughed and took out a piece of paper and said, 'I would now like to say a few words about the deceased.' And this is how his speech went:

People of Lightning Ridge, g-day. We have come together here today to celebrate the lives of Pobby and Dingan, two close mates of Kellyanne Williamson. They have brought much pleasure to our hearts and what a sad loss it is to say our final goodbyes to them — whom many of us never even saw, but only felt. We recall with pleasure Dingan's calm pacifist nature, her opal bellybutton and her pretty face, and many of us will remember Pobby's limp and his generous heart, and let us give thanks for their lives which, whatever anyone says, they most certainly lived.

Well, people were sniffing and taking out handker-
chiefs already. And even some of those real legend, tough
miners were weeping on to the backs of their hands, and
taking out rags covered in dirt to blow their noses into. The
preacher raised his hand and pointed out at the crowd. He
turned up the volume on his voice:

And there are some of you here today who have not believed!
You have not believed in the invisible because it does not
shine forth from the earth and sell for thousands of dollars!
And there are many of you here who have not believed in Pobby
and Dingan. But God believes in them. And he believes in
you. Yup. He sure believes in everyone here. Oh, yes indeedee.
And we are invisible. We are invisible and transparent and
shallow and yet God believes in us. And God believes in Pobby
and Dingan and he is in every single one of those lollies they
sucked and was with them on the school bus, and when they
played rigaragaroo and when they danced in the lightning,
and even, I tell you, when they went missing so tragically
out at the Wyoming Claim where Kellyanne and her brother
Ashmol and their honest dad Rex Williamson went looking
for them. God was with Pobby and Dingan and is still with
them in Heaven. Amen.

Well, thank God the preacher didn't go on for too
long after that! He just said some things about Kellyanne
and what a brave girl she was and he said I was a plucky

kid for sticking up for Pobby and Dingan and fighting for them to have a proper burial. And there was more clapping and my dad slapped me on the back so hard he almost knocked my teeth out. And then the preacher gave himself a more serious look and shouted out something about how if anyone had any reason why Pobby and Dingan should not be buried in the cemetery for them to step forward and say it now. And there was a long silence and I held my breath. And during the silence I was looking around at all these people trying to fix them with my eyes so they wouldn't budge. But then a bloke called Andy Floom stepped forward and everyone turned and looked at him. And the preacher said, 'Well, Andy Floom, speak up!' But Andy Floom, who was a few stubbies short of a six-pack, looked confused and said, 'What? Oh, sorry everyone, I was just, like, stepping forward to squash a spider.' And people started laughing everywhere. And the preacher said OK, now he'd go on with the burial.

So me and Dad and Mum and a few others got down and lifted the coffins into the grave and Kellyanne watched us silently and totally wide-eyed. And only when we had the coffins all lined up in the dark hole did the preacher say, 'Ashes to ashes and dust to dust,' and tears start glimmering down her face. And then I pushed Kellyanne forward in her wheelchair and she placed in the grave a whole pack of Cherry Ripes and Violet Crumbles, a couple of books and things. And Mum put in some flowers and then we stood in silence while two miners shovelled in some soil like they did when they filled in a mine shaft that wasn't being used no more. And when the coffins were covered and buried the preacher led a prayer, and after that everybody started walking slowly home sniffing into their sleeves. And I walked out last with my dad resting his hand on my shoulder. And on the way out someone stopped us at the gate. It was Old Sid and he was holding out his fists and swaying in the road and shouting, 'Come on, Rex Williamson! Come and fight me, you fucking ratter! You're not going to get away with this! Turning the whole of the Ridge against me, you piece of shit! You ever come trespassing on my claim again and I'll, I'll, I'll k-kill . . . !' But then some kids ran up to him and started shouting, 'Lizard eater! Lizard eater! Old Sid is a lizard eater!' and Sid turned away and we watched them hounding him back up the road as he swiped at them with drunk arms.

Dad and I caught up Mum and Kellyanne on the road. Well, Mum was suddenly smiling and singing out that it was about time we menfolk got back to mining, because she reckoned it wouldn't be too long before we found something. And me and Dad looked at each other and couldn't believe those words came out of her mouth. And as we came up to them, Mum turned the wheelchair around to show us that Kellyanne was smiling too. And Kellyanne Williamson smiled for the rest of her life.

*   *   *

But her life was short. A week later the whole population of Lightning Ridge came out to the cemetery again. My sister Kellyanne Williamson was buried with her imaginary friends in the same grave in the same place where millions of years ago there had been sea and creatures swimming cheerfully around. And she took with her some Violet Crumbles in case Pobby and Dingan had run out.

And although in the end everyone believed that Pobby and Dingan had really lived and were really dead, nobody at the Ridge could quite believe the funeral of Kellyanne Williamson was actually happening. And I, Ashmol, still can't believe that it did. I just can't. I can't believe it at all. Even now, one year later, it feels like she's still totally alive. And I find myself lying awake talking to her all the time. And I talk to her at school and when I am walking down Opal Street; and Humph and I when we are out at the Moozeum talk to her together, and if you go to Lightning Ridge today you will still see people pause in the middle of doing whatever they are doing to stop and talk to Kellyanne Williamson just as they still pause to talk to Pobby and Dingan and to opal in their dreams. And the rest of the world thinks we are all total nutters, but they can go and talk to their backsides for all I care. Because they are all just fruit-loops who don't know what it is to believe in something which is hard to see, or to keep looking for something which is totally hard to find.

SPECKS IN THE SKY

Ben Rice was born in Devon in 1972. He read
English at Newcastle University and Oxford.
Ben won the 2001 Somerset Maugham Award.
He lives in London.

Ben Rice

SPECKS IN THE SKY

V

VINTAGE

Thanks to my family and friends and to Bill Buford and Cressida
Leyshon for their helpful suggestions.

Published by Vintage 2002

2 4 6 8 10 9 7 5 3 1

Pobby and Dingan first published in book form in 2000 by
Jonathan Cape

Vintage
Random House, 20 Vauxhall Bridge Road,
London SW1V 2SA

Random House Australia (Pty) Limited
20 Alfred Street, Milsons Point, Sydney,
New South Wales 2061, Australia

Random House New Zealand Limited
18 Poland Road, Glenfield,
Auckland 10, New Zealand

Random House South Africa (Pty) Limited
Endulini, 5A Jubilee Road, Parktown 2193, South Africa

The Random House Group Limited Reg. No. 954009
www.randomhouse.co.uk

A CIP catalogue record for this book is available from the British Library

ISBN 0 09 928562 2

Papers used by Random House are natural, recyclable products
made from wood grown in sustainable forests. The manufacturing
processes conform to the environmental regulations of the
country of origin

Typeset by Palimpsest Book Production Limited,
Polmont, Stirlingshire

Printed and bound in Australia by
Griffin Press

FOR PHILIP TRAILL

One morning, two hundred and twenty-five days after my father left home, specks appeared in the huge blue sky over our house. They were tiny and red at first, like pinpricks of blood. Then the specks grew larger, shivered, turned pink, and spread out like firecrackers. They moved farther apart and then appeared to stop and double back on themselves, as if they had changed their minds about something important.

We stood waiting – Mom, Aileen and I, staring at the sky and shielding our eyes from the sun.

'Parachutes,' I said.

'Impossible, darling,' my mother said. 'We're on no flight paths.'

But a few moments later she saw that I was right.

'Jesus! They are, too,' she said. 'Look, Aileen! Parachutes!'

'What the hell are parachutes doing way out here?' asked Aileen.

The parachutes were getting bigger all the time. Already, we could see that the leader was wearing a red jumpsuit, black knee-high boots, and a white crash

helmet. Another thirty seconds, and I could make out his moustache.

'Look at him go!' I yelled.

He made a beautiful long sweeping arch out over the chicken coops, boomeranged in over the roof of the house, lifting his feet to avoid kicking the TV antenna, and came down heavily, perhaps more heavily than he had expected, in our front yard. He went running along past the gaps in the camel-shed wall, his feet sending up clouds of dust, swerved to avoid the bird Jacuzzi, slalomed between the life-size wooden replica of Lawrence of Arabia and the dried-up oasis water feature, and then, just when we thought he was about to fall, righted himself. The pink parachute floated down and swallowed him up like a huge tongue.

The three of us looked at each other, uncertain what to do. And then all of us ran into the front yard.

'Ryder, go help him!' shouted my mother, who was a worrier by nature. 'Get the parachute off. He's going to suffocate.'

I went over and lifted up one side, but, just as I was about to duck underneath, the parachutist came out from under the other side, carrying his helmet under his arm.

He was tall, with black hair parted on the left, and he had broad shoulders and eyes the colour of the sky.

'Afternoon, young missy,' the parachutist said, saluting me and clicking his heels together. 'Allow me to introduce myself. I am Commander Kyle Cheshire.'

2

'Cool,' I said, staring this huge man up and down. 'I'm Ryder Jarvis and I'm a girl.' My mother had instructed me to say 'I'm a girl' when I met new people, owing to the fact that they tended to mistake me for a boy. I have short hair, you see, and a good scowl, and I throw rocks extremely hard and far and from the elbow.

We shook hands.

'I can see you're surprised to see me, little one,' the parachutist said. 'But, if it's any consolation, I sure am surprised to see you, too.'

I felt a cold shadow cross my face and a breeze run through my hair. Our chickens began squawking in their coops and our camels were braying. Nellie, our dog, ran around the yard barking and jumping up and down.

'Watch out, little lady!' the Commander shouted. 'Here comes Bud!'

I ducked and put my hands over my head. The next thing I knew, there was a thud behind me. I turned around, and a second parachutist emerged from underneath his chute.

'Bud! Good landing! Nicely taken, pal. Nice toggle control.'

'Thanks, Commander,' shouted Bud, who was also a tall, good-looking man with a jaw like a shovel. 'I thought I was bird feed for a moment up there.'

Bud was younger and slightly skinnier than the Commander, and his ears were a little sticky-outy. He looked

3

up to the sky. 'Looks like everyone got out in time, Commander,' he said.

'Got out of where?' my mother called.

The Commander walked over and introduced himself with a low bow. 'Delighted to meet you, ma'am,' he said. 'You must be the proprietor of this remote homestead. May I just say it's a real pleasure to have landed on the property of so handsome a woman.'

My mother's mouth dropped open about as wide as a parachute.

'And these must be your precious daughters,' the Commander said, bowing even lower to my sister Aileen. 'My, oh, my! We seem to have touched down on an island of goddesses. Isn't that right, Bud?'

Bud wasn't listening, though. He was staring at the sky. 'Boy,' he said, 'I sure hope Chip made it.'

'Relax, Bud,' the Commander said. 'Chip is a good man, the best on the team. If Chip Gainsborough didn't make it, nobody did.'

And everybody did seem to be making it. There were more thuds and grunts, and more pink parachutes in all corners of our yard. The parachutists wore identical red jumpsuits with white helmets, and they all carried pistols in their holsters.

I darted about, introducing myself and giving the parachutists high fives. They were saying things like 'Phew!' and 'Son of a gun!' and 'That was a mighty close shave!'

One of them said, 'Man, oh, man. The baby just totally blew up. Next thing I know, I'm in free fall.' Another said, 'God bless America!'

Meanwhile, Bud was rushing around asking about Chip. 'Anyone see him on the descent?' he said.

'Not since the cockpit.'

'Gee whiz! No Chip, then?'

Aileen came over and put her hand on my shoulder and together we watched Bud. 'Anyone hook up with Chip on the way down?' he kept asking.

'Poor thing,' Aileen said. 'He's so anxious about his friend.'

The moment she spoke, the parachutists stopped what they were doing, realizing they were in the presence of a real beauty, with long dark hair and breasts and everything.

One of them walked over, took hold of Aileen's hand, and got down on one knee. 'Pretty lady,' he said, 'if I were still single, I'd make my chute into a wigwam of love and woo you into it with a poem.'

Aileen, who had never had this kind of attention from such a handsome man before, didn't know where to look.

'That's my sister Aileen,' I piped up, coming to her rescue. 'She's nearly sixteen. And my name's Ryder, and I'm also, just for the record, a girl.'

'You're a cool kid, Ryder,' one of them said. 'I dig the tomboy thing you got going there!'

'Thanks,' I said. 'But, actually, it's kinda temporary. When I grow up, I'm gonna grow my hair long and have massive breasts and boyfriends and everything.'

They all laughed, and then the Commander shouted, 'Okay, men. Fall in, everyone!'

The parachutists shouted, 'Yes, sir!' Those who were still attached to their parachutes unhitched themselves, and fourteen parachutists assembled in two rows just in front of our house, standing with their arms flat against their sides in a sort of triangular formation. They looked like a set of bowling pins.

The Commander scrutinized his men, coughed, said, 'At ease, fellas,' and took a notepad and a silver-capped pen from the top pocket of his jumpsuit.

'Bud?'

'Yes, sir!'

'Hank?'

'Here!'

'Bill?'

'You got it!'

'Bob?'

'Yup!'

'Jay?'

'Present and correct!'

'Jake?'

'By the skin o' my teeth!'

'Mike?'

6

'Wouldn't have missed it for the world!'

'Chip?'

Silence. The Commander looked up and down the rows of his men.

'Chip? Chip Gainsborough?'

Another silence.

'Chip not down?'

'Oh, my God,' I heard Bud whisper. 'I had a terrible feeling Chip wasn't going to make it.'

'No Chip Gainsborough, then?' the Commander said solemnly, tapping his pen on his front teeth. 'Shoot! That's not good.' He sighed and reluctantly drew a cross on his notepad.

'Maybe he just got swept off course,' I called out.

The fifteen parachutists turned in unison.

'Sh-h-h! Ryder,' my mom said. 'Don't interrupt.'

'That's a real nice sentiment, young lady,' the Commander called over. 'But unfortunately it's impossible. In a Force 10, sure, my men can miss the zone, but in this case, no. We do not tolerate that degree of inaccuracy in this outfit. I'm afraid the truth is that Chip's chute must have failed to open. Very possibly, the rip on his backup jammed, too.'

The air suddenly felt tense.

'Yes, the truth is that Chip has raspberry-pancaked,' said the Commander solemnly.

'I beg your pardon?' said my mother. 'What do you mean, raspberry pan—' Then she realized what it meant.

7

Bud raised his face to the sky. 'Chip! Chip!' he hollered. 'Don't do this to me, man!' He collapsed on his knees on the hot earth. I looked up at the sky again – just in case.

But the sky was empty. There were no more specks.

For the next fifteen minutes or so, Mom, Aileen and I stood watching as the parachutists went around hugging each other and trying to cheer up Bud. They slapped him on the back, saying, 'Hang in there, Bud!' and 'We're with you, man!' and 'Courage, big fella!'

Bud said that he and Chip had grown up together. 'He was like a brother to me,' he said, on the verge of tears. 'Like a big brother. We used to share everything, man. We collected soda cans for the deposit and bought our first basketball together.'

Eventually, the dashing Commander came over and clapped Bud on the shoulder. 'Bud,' he said, 'you can be proud of Chip. The best ones die young, we all know that. But the cruel truth is that someday, Bud, we will all take a jump and our chutes won't open. One day, all of us will find that our rip cords have jammed and that there is nothing before us but a terrifying plummet onto hard, unforgiving ground.'

My mom came forward, and the men politely made way for her. They took off their helmets and arranged them on the ground, where they sparkled in the sun like a batch of giant eggs.

'I don't mean to interrupt you, men,' she said. 'It's a terrible thing that's happened to your colleague, don't get me wrong, a really soul-destroying thing. But I am the owner of this property and I have my responsibilities. So would one of you gentlemen now care to give me some sort of an explanation?'

The men looked at each other, bemused.

'Forgive me,' the Commander said. 'I'm not sure I follow.'

'Well, Commander,' my mother said, a little impatiently, 'follow this: It's nine in the morning and you come parachuting right in here without a word about what you're doing. But you must know as well as I do that planes never fly over these parts. Never. I mean, take a look around you. Does this look like a place used to receiving visitors?'

The parachutists turned and looked at our rickety old weatherboard house with the patched-up windows and the lopsided sign saying 'Jarvis Camel Safaris'. They looked at Lawrence of Arabia and our two camels, who were lying down under the sparse shade of the elephant tree. They cast their eyes over the cramped cacti standing with their hands on their hips like old men complaining about the weather, and saw all my father's junk, which was scattered about the place: his ant factory, the rusty camel-riding simulator, the gecko maze and the chewing-gum sculpture. They could see how arid everything was and how dilapidated and miserable and run down. They turned around and

surveyed the nothingness beyond our rotting fence: the long dirt roads, the wide-open plains and the huge, butt-naked sky.

'Well, I hear what you're saying, ma'am,' the Commander said, cupping her hand in his as though it were a hamster. 'The situation is this: Following the activation of the emergency signal in our craft, and following the arrival of insurmountable circumstances, we were compelled to activate our emergency procedure and eject at twenty-five thousand feet. We then began falling through freezing temperatures at a hundred and ten miles per hour in a gravity-induced plummet.'

'Go on,' my mother said.

'Having spotted your isolated dwelling during free fall, I designated your yard as a potential drop zone, and thus steered a course toward it. After relaying my intentions to the team, we gained our emergency objective. Now, however,' the Commander continued, and his voice cracked and wobbled. 'Now, however, ma'am, we have arrived on your property only to discover we are one man short. And not just one ordinary man, either. One important man. One American. One Chip.'

I made a clicking noise with my tongue. My mother was staring at her feet as though they were two rabbits she had run over on the road.

'I'm sorry, Commander,' my mother said. 'It must be awful for you having lost one of your men, just awful. But

who are you? Army? Navy? Special Forces? Some kind of fairground display team? You haven't even said. You've simply appeared out of nowhere.'

'I'm afraid, ma'am,' the Commander said, 'we are not at liberty to divulge this information at present.'

'Not at liberty?'

'No, ma'am. That is, it's classified. Only one other person knows the precise nature of the very important mission we embarked upon, and that is the man whose orders we were following. The great man who commissioned our noble project.'

'You mean the President himself?'

'Once more, ma'am, I am afraid that information is classified. But I can reassure you that we will be acting lawfully under the terms and conditions outlined in Section 15 of the *Parachuting Handbook*, 'Landing Upon Civilian Property', clause number 33B, where it states explicitly that we are to assist the said civilians in any way we can during our stay on the civilian premises.'

'You mean you're staying here?'

The Commander smiled and said that, yes, with my mother's permission, he and his men would be staying with us until they had studied their maps, relocated the body of their colleague Chip Gainsborough, and considered it safe to relaunch their mission. 'And, therefore, in the meantime,' he said stroking his sleek moustache, 'I wonder if, having already stunned us with your beauty,

you would now be kind enough to quench the thirst of fifteen bereaved but ultimately optimistic parachutists.'

Once inside the kitchen, the parachutists sat, some on chairs, some on the floor, whispering among themselves, and pointing at things as though they were inside a church.

'Wow!' one said.

'Spectacular!' said another.

'I adore your lazy Susan,' said another. 'My mother had one just like it.'

I went out back to fetch a case of beer, and Aileen got down as many glasses and mugs as she could find in our cupboards. There were only fourteen, and so she poured one can into a bowl.

'This is a mighty fine place you have here, ma'am, if you don't mind me saying,' one of the parachutists said. It may have been the one called Lyle.

'Thank you, young man,' my mom said, 'but I am afraid it's not true. We have lived in chaos ever since our business folded.'

'No, no,' Lyle continued. 'Honestly, ma'am. It makes me wish we had to bail out of our plane every day!'

My mother laughed nervously, and the laughter spread right around the kitchen in a circle, and before long all of the parachutists were laughing – apart from Bud. When the enormous laugh had finished, Bud stood up, raised his beer, and said solemnly, 'To Chip! My long-lost buddy. May he rest in peace.'

'We will look for Chip's body in due course,' the Commander announced. 'And I assure you that, once found, he will be given a parachutist's burial, with full ceremonial honours.'

Then he stood up on a chair and said, 'Gentlemen, your orders for this morning are as follows: you will help this fine woman and her wonderful daughters with the housework and any chores that might need doing about the place.'

'Oh, that won't be necessary, Commander,' said my mom. 'Really. I have two perfectly capable girls here.'

'Madam,' the Commander said, holding up his palms, 'sit back and relax. Our superior saw to it that my men were trained in domestic affairs. Please do not stand in their way.'

And, with that, the parachutist named Luke rolled up his sleeves and began clearing the glasses. He stacked them in two columns, as if he'd been waiting tables his whole life, and carried them to the kitchen sink, while another man, Rob, I believe, stood by his side, his dishrag poised, like a ball player with a mitt.

'Please, don't, gentlemen,' my mother said, unable to suppress a smile. 'This kind of thing is woman's work.'

'Ma'am, with all respect, this is the twenty-first century,' the Commander said. 'Our superior is nothing if not a modern man and a staunch feminist. It is what he expects of us.'

'Madam, could you direct me to a vacuum cleaner?' called out a man who looked a little like Tom Cruise and who I'm pretty sure was named Mart.

'No, honestly,' said my mother, clutching her forehead. 'Please, don't, gentlemen. You'll put me to shame.'

Just then, one of the parachutists, whose name was Greg, stepped forward. 'Ahem,' he said. 'Excuse me, ma'am, but would you mind me asking if there is a man currently living in the house?'

My mother's eyebrow twitched like a lizard's tail.

'Only, we could heartily do with some tools, ma'am,' Greg said. 'That's not to say, ma'am, of course, that a woman would not necessarily be in charge of the tools, but often it works the other way around, and so I was just wondering if there might at present be a man in the house who might direct me toward some tools.'

There was a terrible silence. I looked at Aileen. Aileen bit her lip and looked at the floor.

'No,' my mom said. 'There is no man. That is to say, there was once, but not any more.'

The Commander nodded and looked grave.

'I'm sorry to hear that, ma'am. My colleague Greg here was not meaning to pry. Life, as I have said with regard to Chip Gainsborough, is darn short. One minute we are here. The next minute we are six feet under, our bodies fast food for the worms. But we have pride, ma'am. We

14

have pride in our dying, just the same. And I'm sure when your husband died—'

'My husband didn't die!' my mom said, sounding louder than she had intended. 'He left! Okay? He just left!'

There was a collective sigh of empathy from the parachutists, followed by a chorus of 'Typical, typical'. I thought for a minute that my mom was going to cry.

'There are tools out in the shed, Commander Cheshire,' I said. 'They're brand new. Mom bought them for my dad's birthday, but he never got around to using them.'

'Perfect, young Ryder,' the Commander said. 'Well, if you would escort me to your car, ma'am, I will give it a tune up. Or did your husband take the car when he went?'

'Yes, he did,' said my mother, who had regained some of her composure. 'But the pickup is still here in the garage and could heartily do with some attention.'

'Show me to it,' the Commander said. 'And show us your scorched flower beds and one of the boys will see them restored to perfection. We have a qualified landscape jardinier on the team.'

Within seconds, the fifteen parachutists clicked into action. One man was under the pickup, another up a stepladder repairing the hole in the living-room ceiling. A few more began helping my mother heave Lawrence of Arabia and the bird Jacuzzi and the rest of my dad's junk into a pile at

the side of the yard. Meanwhile, two men announced their intention to conduct a 'systematic shopping excursion'.

'But the nearest store is five miles away,' my mother said. 'And you can't go like that. People around here are not used to seeing men in red jumpsuits. Word will get out, and before you know it—'

'Excellent point,' the Commander said. 'You have an instinct for management. A natural gift. We can't possibly have anyone knowing that we are here. We must conduct ourselves with the maximum discretion at all times.'

It was decided that my mother would provide the men with my dad's old clothes. She had hung on to them, saying that one day they might come in handy, if we ever had men of our own. Not, she said, that she'd recommend it.

The clothes were musty and smelled of cigarettes and beer and my dad's overpowering body odour – he had taken to using deodorant and soap only on special occasions. Anyway, we got them for the men, and then Mom, Aileen and I left the room while the parachutists changed.

While we were waiting, Mom whispered, 'I can't believe this is happening.'

'It's pretty unreal,' said Aileen.

'I reckon there's something weird going on,' I said. 'They must be escaped criminals. Or aliens or something.'

'You watch too many movies, Ryder,' my mother said.

16

'These men are clearly an important team of professionals who have simply run into troublesome circumstances and are making the best of a bad situation. They're most likely government intelligence agents, and it is our duty as fellow American citizens to accommodate them.'

'I feel really sorry for poor Chip,' Aileen said. 'His body could be anywhere. And his friend Bud, poor thing, is almost desperate with grief.'

'Yes, it's sad,' my mother said. 'But, then again, these are not the kind of men to crack when the going gets rough. These are the tough-cookie type, the kind who take the hard knocks and get on with their lives.'

The door opened and the men filed out into the yard carrying their jumpsuits. On each parachutist, I noticed a piece of my dad's old clothing. His fluorescent belt. His green sweatshirt with the elbow holes. His pair of flared work pants. His 'kiss a camel and taste the difference' baseball cap. His yellow windbreaker. The T-shirt with the Africa-shaped coffee stain and the bits of dried egg down the front.

'Oh, my Lord!' my mother said, clasping her hand to her mouth. 'Have you ever seen anything like it?'

'Are they wearing Dad's underwear, too?' I asked, suddenly embarrassed. I was referring to the baggy white-mesh Y-fronts he used to wear under his bathrobe and loaf around in on Saturday mornings, watching super-hero cartoons. They were so big, those underpants, that you

could have stretched out a single pair between two trees and made a hammock.

'Look!' said Aileen, who was standing with her nose pressed against the window.

On the washing line, there were now fifteen red jumpsuits moving around in the breeze, like a headless pop band. And on the ground the pink parachutes were spread out in the sun to air. I don't think our camels had seen anything so impressive since Dad drove his solar-powered motorscooter through the wall of their shed.

I found the parachutist called Greg near the washing machine. 'Don't worry, young miss,' he said, nodding at the bras, stockings and panties he had collected in his arms. 'I've seen it all before. I'm married myself, with three teenage daughters. There's not a negligee in North America that would bring the colour to my cheeks!'

'So where do your wife and kids live?' I asked him.

'What was that, miss?'

'You mentioned you had kids,' I said. 'And I was wondering where they live.'

'That's a good question,' he answered.

'I know,' I said.

'Well, as a matter of fact, I'm from a picturesque little town not far from Oklahoma City,' he said.

'Oh, yeah?' I asked. 'What town's that?'

'What town, little missy?'

'Yeah, what town?'

'Er . . . St-Stewartsville,' he said, coughing into his hand, and then he returned to the laundry.

I ran upstairs to the room we call the library, which is more or less a couch, a TV and a few shelves of books, and took down the big leather-bound world atlas. My suspicions were correct. Greg the parachuting laundryman had been lying. There was no Stewartsville, Oklahoma. Stewartsville didn't exist. Weird, I thought, but I decided to keep this to myself for a while, until I had made some further observations.

Out in the yard, the parachutist called Mike had set up a makeshift workbench and was sawing pieces of wood and then hammering them together.

'What is it?' I asked him. 'What are you making?'

'Take a guess, kid,' he said.

'Is it a canoe?'

'Good idea,' he said. 'It could be, couldn't it?'

Mike began whooping and hollering and paddling like a maniac, and for ten minutes we chased each other all over.

'For a parachutist, you shoot a pretty mean arrow,' I said.

'Years of practice,' he replied. 'Your pop never played cowboys and Native Americans with you, kid?'

'Sometimes,' I said. 'But not so much. He was usually quite busy with his projects.'

Mike looked over at the pile of Dad's contraptions. 'So what was the point of all those projects?'

'I am afraid I am not at liberty to reveal this information at present,' I said, and walked away, feeling pretty smart.

On the other side of the yard, the parachutist called Bob was giving our camels a health check.

'Don't worry, miss,' Bob said as he inspected their teeth. 'I'm a trained veterinarian. We'll have your *cameli dromedarii* better in no time.'

He shined a torch in their eyes. He looked up their hairy asses. He patted their straggly fawn humps and examined their pairs of toes. And all the time he was saying, 'Hmm, looks like a case of serious neglect.'

'My dad didn't neglect them,' I protested. 'He loved them, he really did. But it's expensive keeping camels, and when they got scabies and the first one died, he . . . Look, he loved those camels more than anything.'

'Yeah, well,' Bob said, 'I guess not enough to stay and look after the survivors, huh?'

I couldn't think of a reply this time, and I still hadn't thought of one when Hank and Mart came back with the shopping.

There were twenty bags altogether, including food for the camels. And sixteen bunches of flowers.

'All these for me?' gasped my mother.

'Only one bunch, I'm afraid, ma'am,' laughed Hank.

'The rest are for Chip. We thought we'd place them with his body when we find him.'

'Of course,' my mother said. 'I'm sorry. How presumptuous of me.'

'Ma'am, may I introduce Big Jay, our cook,' said Commander Cheshire. 'What will you be whipping up for lunch, Jay?'

'Nothing fancy, Commander,' said Big Jay, who was looking through the shopping bags. 'But, if you give me a moment, I should be able to throw together a salmon-asparagus soufflé and cannelloni stuffed with broccoli paste for starters, followed by a pork cutlet on a couch of potatoes importantés, with parsnips and an avocado, thyme and lemon sauce. And, for dessert, a prime Sicilian mango sorbet.'

'Wait. You're cooking this for us?' my mother said.

'Sure am,' said Jay. 'It's really not such a big deal, ma'am. Remember, we have rehearsed for years for exactly this kind of situation. I am hungry to put everything I have practised in my training into operation in the field.'

The Commander slapped Jay on the back and informed his men that it was time to get washed up for lunch.

In a few minutes, a line formed along the landing outside the bathroom. The fifteen tanned parachutists stood patiently with their towels around their waists. One sat on a stool cutting his toenails, collecting the little hard crescents in the lid of a shaving-cream can, which he emptied

out in the wastebasket. Some read books. I noticed that, whereas my dad had always had love handles, and a potbelly that he called his 'hump', these parachutists had no extra fat. They had nipples like little raspberries, and their bodies were hairless except for neat patches of crisp arrow-shaped chest hair pointing down to their you-know-whats.

'What you reading, Jake?' somebody asked.

'A book by a writer named Menjabin. Chip lent it to me yesterday.'

'He did? What's it about?'

'That's a tricky one,' Jake said. 'I guess it's a kind of domestic tragicomedy-cum-Surrealist fable. Menjabin takes potshots at gender self-consciousness and hypocrisy in a post-feminist world.'

'Good for her!' shouted Lyle.

'No, actually, it's a him,' said Jake. 'The author's name is Eric. Eric Menjabin.'

'Oh, right,' said Lyle, 'Well, it sounds awesome, anyway.'

'Actually, it's not,' said Jake. 'His grasp of the American idiom is at best shaky. His understanding of feminism blinkered and naive. The narrative depends upon the same cheap gags endlessly repeated. And, as for his characters' — he took off his tortoiseshell glasses — 'well, to put it bluntly, they're all of them shallow stereotypes. Then again it might just be me,' Jake sighed. 'After losing Chip, books seem a little futile, don't they?'

'You're right, Jake,' the Commander said. 'A tragedy like this makes any work of art seem redundant. What can a frivolous story masquerading as a novel of ideas possibly offer us in the face of human loss?'

'I agree, sir,' Jake went on, flicking through the book. 'Look at this. Chip has underlined his favourite passages. And you see these doodles? How much more meaningful are Chip's last humble scribbles than any of Eric Menjabin's cynical utterances.'

The parachutists crowded in to admire Chip's doodles, and while they were poring over them I tapped Aileen's elbow and we sneaked into the bathroom to wash up without the parachutists noticing.

'My God, these guys are so smart!' Aileen said.

Everything in the bathroom was clean as a whistle. I was wondering what kind of men could possibly be so clean when Aileen let out a scream.

'What is it?' I yelled.

Aileen was staring at the toilet. 'Look. Can you believe it?' she screeched.

'What?' I said.

'They put the seat back down!'

My dad had always left the toilet seat up, of course. He left hairs in the tub, too. They were long and squiggly – like the scrawny handwriting in the message he had put on the kitchen table before he left, which said, 'Your Mom wants me to go and so I'm leaving.'

After we had cleaned up, we went downstairs and waited while the squeaky-clean parachutists, smelling of shaving cream, came down one by one to listen to the local news on the radio. They were relieved to hear no reports of any parachute sightings in the area. This, the Commander told us, meant that the secrecy of their mission was still intact, and that once they had recovered Chip they could pick up right where they had left off.

'Lunch is served, everyone!' Jay called from the kitchen.

We marched in and the parachutists formed an orderly line at the stove. They waited until everyone had filled their plates, and then sat down and took up their knives and forks and the Commander said, 'For what we are about to receive, may God, Allah, Buddha, the Hindu Trimurti, or whoever rules our own personal religious world make us truly thankful.'

'Amen,' the men said.

'And Awomen, too,' added the Commander.

There was silence but for the smacking of lips. Unlike my father, who really loved a good chew, the parachutists ate silently, with their mouths closed. And they didn't slurp their wine. They sipped it, and drew comparisons between the taste and things like freshly mowed grass in the summer, or bonfire smoke, or lavender and honey and driftwood.

'May I say once again, ma'am, your elder daughter is

as pretty as pecan pie,' the Commander said between mouthfuls. 'And the younger will break hearts when she's grown out of that tomboy phase.'

'Thank you, sir,' my mom said. 'I've done my best to bring them up to be resourceful, sensible girls. But it has been hard with no man in the house to help me with their education.'

'You have had great success, nevertheless, ma'am,' the Commander said. 'I am only too aware of how tough it can be running a household solo, for my wife left me ten years ago.'

My mother and the Commander then exchanged what I can only describe as a deep and meaningful look. I don't know about the Commander, but I know my mother was trying to imagine what kind of woman would be crazy enough to walk out on a man like this. Maybe there was something else on her mind, too. Anyway, for the rest of the meal she remained strangely quiet and glanced up only once or twice from her food.

There was a loud beeping sound and the Commander reached into the pocket of my dad's pants, took out a watch, turned off the alarm, and blew on a silver whistle.

'Gentlemen,' he said, 'now that you are replenished, it is time to return to serious matters. We must immediately conduct a thorough search for Chip Gainsborough before the birds attempt to gorge themselves upon his body.'

The parachutists marched outside, and one of them got

behind the wheel of the pickup and seven others clambered up into the back and sat opposite each other on the benches, knee to knee. They loaded on bottles of water, covered themselves in sunscreen, and lifted onto their laps the strange-shaped canoe.

'Hey, why are you taking the canoe, Mike?' I asked.

'It's no canoe, little one,' Mike said. 'Actually, it's a coffin to put our colleague Chip in once we find him.'

I felt stupid for not figuring it out, and a little spooked because I had been playing cowboys and Indians in a coffin without even knowing it.

'Good luck, men,' the Commander said. 'Keep your eyes peeled at all times.'

'Take Nellie with you,' Aileen said. 'She has a wicked sense of smell.'

'Can I go, too?' I asked.

'That's a nice idea, young miss,' the Commander said, 'but, in this case, no, you may not.'

'How come?' I said.

The Commander squatted down so he was at my level and smiled at me sadly. 'Well, pretty missy,' he said, 'because the sight of a dead parachutist is too much for a young lady to bear.'

'I don't mind,' I said.

'I believe you,' the Commander said. 'But, remember, Chip hit the ground at a great velocity. He may well have

become dismembered on impact. His head may have rolled some distance from his neck, and his eyeballs will have definitely become dislodged.'

'I think it's best we stay at home, then, Ryder, don't you?' said my mother.

'You will be in good company, ladies,' the Commander said. 'For seven of us will stay here and help make preparations for the funeral. And we will start by digging a grave for Chip Gainsborough in the yard.'

'A grave?' I said.

'In our yard?' said my mother. 'But surely Chip's parents will want his body flown home.'

'That's a lovely sentiment, ma'am,' the Commander said. 'But Chip's parents died two years ago, and besides, it's a tradition in our outfit that, following an accident of this kind, a parachutist must be buried in close proximity to the said site of impact.'

'But you can't bury him here,' I said. 'We don't even know him.'

'Don't worry about that, miss,' the Commander said. 'I can assure you that Chip would have felt very comfortable in these quiet yet domestic surroundings. He was a country boy himself. And, knowing how proud his parents were of his profession, I feel confident that to be buried here near the said site of impact is exactly what they would have wanted for him.'

Then he turned to the men in the pickup. 'Godspeed,

boys! And be as quick as you can, for we have a great deal to prepare before tonight.'

'Now,' the Commander said, after the pickup had disappeared along the dirt road. 'Like the great American poet, we find ourselves in a proverbial yellow wood.'

'What?' I said.

'We have two options. Which would you prefer to do: arrange the flowers for Chip's funeral or dig the trench?'

'Are you kidding?' I said.

My mother, Aileen and I crossed the yard to the shed to fetch the pickaxe and the shovels while the remaining parachutists went inside the house to put together a few funeral bouquets for Chip.

'Right, girls,' my mother said. 'We must grant the dead privacy. So we'll dig at the bottom of the yard, well away from the house.'

I guess it's not every mother who can handle a pickaxe. But mine, underneath her fragile exterior, was tough as boots. The ground was dry and rock-hard, but Mom just clenched her teeth and raised the pickaxe and then hurled it down. And, after a few hard blows, the earth started to give.

'He's cracking!' my mother yelled. 'We've got him on the ropes, girls!'

She put down her pick and wiped the sweat from her forehead.

'Nothing like a little womanual labour, huh?' she smiled.

Then we took up our shovels and started digging. We hadn't been working long before Mom and Aileen started rattling on and on about how wonderful the parachutists were. I decided now was a good time to spill the beans about Stewartsville, Oklahoma.

'So what? That doesn't necessarily add up to anything, Ryder,' Aileen said. 'His home town is probably too small to be covered by our atlas.'

'Now, listen here, honey,' my mother said. 'I know that this is hard to believe, and that in the past I have often said otherwise, but you have to understand that not every man in the world is a liar.'

'I'm not saying all men are liars,' I said. 'I'm just saying I've got a hunch these guys—'

'Well, personally, I trust them,' said Aileen.

'Just because you have the hots for that guy Bud,' I said, nudging my sister in the ribs.

'I have not!' protested my sister.

'Now, now, Ryder,' my mother said. 'Who Aileen has the hots for is her business. And, besides, how often does one come across men to have the hots for way out here?'

'How often do you see parachutists who cook and do the housework?' I said.

I was shocked when a tear appeared in my mother's eye.

'Poor boojum,' she said. 'I've scarred you for life. After

29

your father, you'll always have a distorted view of men and never trust a single one of them.'

'That's not true,' I said.

'It is,' sniffed my mother. 'If I had only never married him, you would be much more likely to find happiness with a decent one when you grow up.'

'If you had never married him, I wouldn't be alive,' I said. 'End of story.'

'Ryder has a point there, Mom,' Aileen said.

'Anyway, I haven't got a bad opinion of men,' I said. 'I liked Dad. He was a bit lazy, granted, and he had some strange ideas. But generally—'

'Now, don't you "generally" me, Ryder Jarvis,' my mother said, taking up her shovel and plunging it into the soil. 'He took things much too far, and well you know it.'

'She's right, Ryder. He did,' said Aileen.

'He was a failure, pure and simple,' my mother said. 'You only have to look at these parachutists to see that. They have everything he lacked. Common sense. Charm. Discipline. Consistency.'

'Mom has a point,' Aileen said. 'Remember Dad's crazy ideas that always backfired? That lizard-racing syndicate, for example, or the whole camel-trekking business?'

'Come on, it wasn't his fault we lost the camels,' I said.

'Not directly,' my mother said, throwing a shovel's

worth of soil over her shoulder. 'But dragging us out here in the first place was sheer madness – setting up a tourist attraction in the middle of nowhere with no decent roads and zero sightseeing potential.'

'No crazier than digging a trench for someone we don't even know in our own front yard,' I said.

For a second, my mother was at a loss for words.

'Well, at least we're being helpful,' she said. 'Which is more than I could ever say for your father.'

'But Dad's a changed man,' I said. 'He's learned to cook. And he wants to take you on a romantic cruise in his sailboat off the coast of California. He told me on the phone.'

My mother sighed and shook her head. 'No, thanks, Ryder,' she said. 'There's no way in hell I'm going anywhere on a boat that sails against the wind. It's a recipe for disaster, as well as a scientific impossibility.'

I was about to explain how the boat worked, using two propellers, the way Dad had shown me out on the creek with a model, but Mom wasn't listening.

'Men never change, Ryder,' she said. 'Remember that. Now, come on, we should stop wasting time and get on with more practical matters, like digging this here trench for Chip Gainsborough. We don't want the Commander coming out and catching us slacking, do we?'

We finished the trench just before it got dark. Then we went inside, where we discovered that the parachutists had not made a few simple wreaths. Oh, no. They had woven a huge tapestry out of the flowers. In the foreground, the words 'chip gainsborough – rest in peace' were spelled out in chrysanthemums and desert poppies. And if you stared at the word 'chip' long enough more details began to appear. For example, in the 'P' a sky of blue cornflowers emerged dotted with parachutes made from pink roses, and if you closed one eye and stood very close you could just about make out a plane of tulip petals flying through clouds of white gerberas towards a dandelion sun.

'Holy cow!' my mother said. 'It's a work of art.'

'Nothing so glamorous, I'm afraid,' the Commander said. 'But I think Chip would have appreciated it. He had a penchant for trompe l'oeil and a deep respect for floral pentimento.'

He was just explaining what pentimento meant when headlights swept across the walls of the kitchen.

'They're back from the search!' cried Luke.

We rushed to the door. The parachutists jumped from the pickup and, with shouts of 'We did it!', turned cartwheels across the moonlit yard.

'We have recovered Chip's body!' Bud shouted. 'We found him!'

He ran over to Aileen and threw his arms around her

and planted a kiss on her forehead. Mom, meanwhile, was waving at the parachutists as though welcoming them home from war.

The Commander stood proudly on the doorstep, his arms folded across his chest. 'Well done, men!' he cried jubilantly. 'Never let future generations say that you were not the bedfellows of victory and success.' Then he lit a cigar.

The parachutists hugged and playfully punched one another, and Aileen and my mom hugged and punched them, too.

'However,' the Commander went on, puffing hard to get the cigar going, 'let us not forget the gravity of this occasion. For against our gains we must measure our losses. Tonight, a great star has been extinguished. Chip Gainsborough, gentlemen, is dead.'

Everyone was quiet again, and the men unloaded the coffin, grunting under its weight, and, with extreme care, lowered it onto the ground.

'What did Chip look like when you found him?' I asked. 'Was he, like, totally deformed?'

'Sh-h-h, Ryder,' my mother said. 'What kind of a question is that?'

'A perfectly good one, ma'am,' Mike said. 'He was kinda like this, miss.' And he lay down on the ground in order to demonstrate the position in which they had discovered Chip. 'And amazingly well preserved. The

impact of the fall made a crater around him, protecting him from the desert winds.'

'Dust clung to his legs,' Bud added, 'and his parachute lay beside him like a forlorn lover.'

'My, how tragic,' Aileen said.

'No need to be upset, ladies,' the Commander said. 'I assure you that it would have all been over very quickly for Chip. Like switching out the lights. There would have been little time for any pain.' He paused and licked his lips, as if tasting the gravity of the moment. 'Now,' he said gravely. 'Let the funeral proceedings unfold.'

The parachutists laid the magnificent tapestry of flowers down before the coffin and formed themselves in a perfect horseshoe around it. The Commander handed out candles. The flames flickered and swayed in front of their faces.

'May I say, ma'am, how youthful you seem tonight,' the Commander whispered to my mother.

I cringed, but he was right. Mom was not a troubled middle-aged housewife any longer. In the flickering candlelight she looked like a young girl on her first date in a dark movie theatre.

The parachutist called Pete took out a bugle, raised it to his lips, and played 'Taps'. It was, I don't mind admitting, a very moving moment. The bugle glowed in the moonlight. Our chickens were as still on their roosts as china vases on a shelf, and even Nellie sat quietly and listened as the music swelled hypnotically in the desert air.

When Pete had finished, the Commander heeled his cigar into the ground and stepped forward. 'I would like to give thanks for the great – nay, extraordinary – life of Chip Archibald Gainsborough, who joined us on many missions and achieved an array of excellent – nay, astounding – results. He was sensitive, but not overly so. He could be wild and passionate, and cool and rational. He was sophisticated and he was primitive, and both idealistic and practical. And now that his supreme life has come to an end, and his body lies supine before us in this simple wooden vessel, I would like to sum it all up by saying, once more, thank you for the life and times of Chip Gainsborough – the complete man.'

There were nods of approval and murmurs of 'Here, here.' Bud added, in a quavering voice, 'And he was a mighty good buddy to me when I was a kid. We used to dive for sand dollars together. I remember one time up in Maine—' But he broke down and began weeping. And so did Mom.

Meanwhile, I, who had never met the great Chip Gainsborough, and who had been more than a little mistrusting of the parachutists, also felt a tear welling up in the corner of my eye. It occurred to me that I might have been too suspicious of these perfect but warm-hearted parachutists, who had gone to such lengths to recover the corpse of their colleague and see him properly buried. I looked along the row of sad faces, and resolved to give

them the benefit of the doubt and, for the sake of my mother, to cast aside all suspicion. They had, after all, made such an effort to make her happy, and what could possibly be wrong with that? And what did it matter how much she liked the Commander as long as she was still alive?

And then, when all of us were at our most melancholic, we were startled by a terrific swoosh, and the sky was miraculously full of the most magnificent fireworks.

'Wow!' I yelled.

Catherine wheels were whirling on the chicken coops while rockets zipped off skyward, leaving behind a blaze of purple and gold. On the side of the yard, smoke was hissing from a pile of Dad's junk. I thought at first it was fireworks waiting to go off, but a few seconds later the bird Jacuzzi, the chewing-gum sculpture, and poor old Lawrence of Arabia were eaten by flames.

'Hey, wait!' I shouted. 'Who said to burn Lawrence and all Dad's stuff?'

'The Commander,' Mom said. 'And with my blessing. That man's been standing there like a zombie for years, and I'm sick of his useless face.'

'Incredible fireworks!' Aileen yelled. 'But where did they come from?'

'Guilty once again,' the Commander said. 'I can't deny it. I set them up secretly when you were digging.'

'But they'll scare the camels,' I said. 'And Nellie hates loud noises.'

'It's okay, miss. I took the liberty of providing them with earplugs,' said Bob, the parachuting vet.

Meanwhile, the other parachutists whipped sparklers from their pockets, lit them using the candles, and tearfully tried to scribble Chip Gainsborough's name in the air before they fizzled.

'Friends!' the Commander shouted excitedly. 'If I know Chip, and I think I do, he will be looking down upon us right now saying, "Why do they look so sad? Did I live a great and courageous life to be wept over like a broken doll? No! Let there be singing and dancing!"'

'My thoughts exactly, sir!' said Pete, as he came out of the house carrying my father's guitar. 'Life is too short for sadness.'

He began to pluck out a tune, and, with a cry of 'This is for you, Chip!', the Commander grabbed hold of Mom's hand and boogie-woogied off around the yard.

'Come on, miss,' Luke shouted. 'Don't be sad. It's Chip's favourite song!' He pulled me towards him and spun me around and we went careering past Chip's grave. The other parachutists formed a circle, clapping and making whooping noises. 'Yeeehaahh!'

When the song was finally over, the parachutists bowed to us and wiped tears from their eyes and said, 'Ma'am, thank you so much' and 'Chip would be ever so grateful. He was always one for a dance.' I tried to curtsy, but I felt dorky, and so I bowed instead.

Then Bud walked over to the coffin and said, 'Night-night, my brother. And may your pink parachute land you safely in Heaven.'

Four of the parachutists picked up the coffin, raised it carefully onto their shoulders, and carried it to the trench at the bottom of the yard. Just as they were lowering the coffin down to waist level, however, something unexpected happened.

The parachutist named Will, who was holding the front end of the coffin, lost his grip and let out a yelp of panic as he fumblingly tried to recover it. But he couldn't. The coffin slipped from his hands. There was a hollow sound of splintering wood and the parachutists at the rear, shocked by the sudden lurch forward, found their end yanked from their clutches, too. Before they could break the coffin's fall, there was another pine-shattering crunch. The force of the impact swung the lid of the coffin open, exposing the inside for all to see.

For a few seconds, the parachutists stood in a state of spasm, with their shoulders hunched up to their ears. Their faces were screwed up and their eyes squeezed tight.

Because there was nothing inside. Chip Gainsborough's corpse was not there.

We stood gaping at the empty coffin. My mother opened her mouth to say something but no words came. She turned to the Commander for an explanation, but his hands were

clamped over his face as if it were about to crumble into thousands of pieces.

'Commander?' she said.

The Commander let out a long sigh, like the slide of a trombone.

'Commander?' my mother repeated. 'What's going on? Why is Chip Gainsborough not in his coffin?'

'I don't know,' the Commander whispered hoarsely.

'Only I should hate to think, Commander,' my mother continued anxiously, 'that we had gone through all that grieving for poor Chip when his body is still lying unfound and alone somewhere out there.'

The Commander removed his hands, leaving blotchy finger marks on his forehead. He looked at my mother long and hard and then he slowly seemed to pull himself together.

'Good point. My feelings exactly, ma'am,' he said. And he turned sharply to his men.

'Right, men!' he barked. 'You have some explaining to do. Fall in! Fall in immediately! And you better be goddam quick about it!'

The parachutists hastily assembled by the grave in a shaky version of their bowling-pin formation, and glanced sheepishly at one another.

A notch had appeared between the Commander's eyebrows, as if someone had taken a swing at him with a pick.

'Well, now, men,' he said, pacing up and down in front of his men. 'This is some surprise!'

'Yes, sir,' the men mumbled.

'A very unpleasant one, at that,' the Commander went on, and then he started to shout. 'Because, as you are well aware, Chip's body is not in the coffin, where it should be!'

The men said nothing.

'So answer me this, gentlemen,' the Commander continued, in a calmer tone. 'Am I right in thinking that when you came back in triumph bearing Chip Gainsborough's body earlier on you had not in fact found the body at all?'

The parachutists glanced at each other and nodded reluctantly.

'I see,' the Commander said, trying very hard to keep his cool. 'Now, I wonder if I might be so bold as to inquire as to which of you is responsible for this. Who is the ringleader?'

No one answered.

'Very well. In that case, I shall count to fifteen. And if the person who is responsible does not come forward, I will assume you are all culpable and punish the whole outfit.'

The Commander counted to eight quite slowly. No one came forward.

'Nine.' He moved threateningly towards his men. 'Ten, eleven.'

Bud clenched his teeth. Hank closed his eyes as if in prayer.

'Twelve, thirteen, fourteen, fifteen!'

'It was me, sir!'

The parachutist named Lyle took one brave step forward.

The remaining thirteen parachutists sighed with relief.

'It was all my idea, sir,' Lyle said, holding his chin high. 'All my fault, sir. And I would just, sir, like to express my sincere apologies, sir, to you, sir, and this family, sir, for what I have done. I accept full responsibility for the deception, sir.'

The Commander stared at Lyle and shook his head in disgust. He walked over to the young parachutist and squared up to him, chin to chin. Lyle bit his lip and returned the Commander's stare.

'Well, well, well. Lyle Spackman.'

'Yes, sir.'

'Who'd have thought it, eh?'

'I don't know, sir.'

'Well, now, Lyle,' the Commander drawled. 'May I, with your kind permission, be so rude as to ask why you found it necessary to pretend to have found Chip Gainsborough's body?'

Lyle eyed his fellow parachutists, and then, in a throaty whisper, he said, 'Because we thought you might be pretty angry, sir, if we did not find the body, sir, knowing what a

perfectionist you are, sir, and knowing, sir, how important it is to you that a job gets finished properly, and that everything always goes perfect and swimmingly, sir.'

'Is that right? Well, things aren't going too goddam swimmingly now, are they, Lyle Spackman?'

'No, sir.'

'You have made me look like a moron, Lyle. You have made all of us look ridiculous in front of this excellent woman and her family.'

'Yes, sir.'

'Now, this parachute troop prides itself on what, exactly, Lyle?'

'Perfection, sir!'

'Correct,' the Commander said. 'Turn around and put your hands on your head, Lyle Spackman!' he shouted. 'Now!'

Lyle did as he was ordered.

'Have you anything you wish to say before you are dismissed?'

'Not really, sir,' Lyle said, choking up. 'I'd just like to say so long to the fellas. And thank you for being good buddies. And thanks to this family for their hospitality. And I'm really heartily sorry I tried to deceive you, sir.'

'Wait a minute, there, Commander,' my mother said, stepping forward. 'Lordy, there's really no need to go and fire this young man from the outfit. What he did

was wrong, sure. But it sounds like he was only trying to please you. He had your best interests at heart.'

The Commander put a hand on my mother's shoulder. 'Relax, ma'am,' he said, 'and have no fear. I assure you that under no circumstances would I dream of doing such a thing.'

'But you said something about dismissing him,' my mother said. 'Didn't you?'

At that moment, the Commander whipped the pistol from his holster and aimed the barrel straight at Lyle's head. We gasped in astonishment as, holding the gun steady, he placed the nub up against the young parachutist's temple.

'Correct, ma'am, I did,' the Commander said.

'No!' Aileen screamed. 'Commander! What are you doing?'

'Don't do this, please!' my mother howled. 'I beg you! Commander Cheshire! Put that gun away.'

'Stand aside, please, ma'am. And let this man be punished. For this pathetic specimen, this Lyle Spackman, has sought to undermine my authority and make a mockery of our emotions. And it is time to teach him that we do not tolerate fraud in this outfit.'

'You're not serious,' my mother said. 'Tell me this is just some silly parachutist's prank!'

But the Commander wasn't listening.

'Where there is imperfection and lack of respect, where

there is dishonesty and deceit, we weed it out, ma'am. We are a team of consummate professionals. We are not failed camel-keepers who drop everything and walk away when a situation becomes difficult.'

'Please,' Lyle said. 'Let the Commander kill me, ma'am. It is nothing more than I deserve.'

'What are you talking about? You don't deserve to die, Lyle!' screeched Aileen. 'Bud! Do something!'

But Bud just stood there.

We rushed over to the Commander and tried to pull down his arm.

'I said you couldn't trust them, Mom,' I cried. 'I told you they weren't what they seemed.'

'Shut up, you little transvestite!' the Commander said. 'Do you hear? Or I will execute you on the spot!'

I shut up.

'Lyle Spackman,' the Commander said, 'you have pretended that there was a man in a coffin, and now you will, in the most real sense, take up residency in that coffin yourself.'

'I'm ready, sir,' Lyle said.

'Please!' screamed my mother. 'Don't shoot!'

But it was too late. There was a loud whip-crack and Lyle's brains flew from the side of his head like a ball of spit. His legs gave out from underneath him and a thick brown substance oozed from his head onto the ground, where almost instantly it clotted and congealed. I saw it

all from between my fingers, which were covering my face. He buckled and keeled over, twitched, and then lay suddenly still.

The parachutists stared down at Lyle's body. Aileen was bent over, retching. I don't know what Mom was doing. My eyes had misted over, and my left leg was shaking uncontrollably.

After the pistol shot, things seemed to unfold in slow motion. The parachutists' voices were warped and tinny in my ears.

'Well? Is he dead?' I heard the Commander say.

One of the parachutists strode over slowly, like a spaceman, and checked.

'Yes, sir, he's dead, sir. Bullet entered the back of the head, sir. Killed no doubt immediately on impact, sir.'

'Perfect,' said the Commander, licking his lips. 'A satisfactory execution.'

My mother and Aileen were locked in an embrace, whimpering quietly. Perhaps because my legs had turned to jelly, I found myself unable to join them.

'Let that be a lesson to you all, men,' the Commander said. 'Now, clean the traitor up and place him in the coffin, where he belongs!'

No one moved.

'Do as I say!' the Commander screamed, waving his gun at the men. 'Or you will suffer the same punishment.'

Four men came forward. One got down on his knees and

began to sponge Lyle's head wound. One applied shaving cream to his face, took a razor from his pocket, and shaved Lyle's chin. A third lifted his arms and sprayed deodorant under them, while the fourth took out a tie and began to feed it around Lyle's neck.

'Stop this!' yelled my mother. 'He's dead. What the hell are you doing?'

'You know me, ma'am,' the Commander said. 'I will not have my men looking shabby under any circumstances.'

The parachutists folded Lyle's arms across his chest and carried him to the coffin.

'And never let it be said,' shouted the Commander, 'that our punishments do not fit our crimes, either.'

But the parachutists were having some trouble fitting Lyle into the coffin.

'He's too tall, sir!' they called.

'What?'

'We can't fit Lyle in, sir,' explained Mike, who had made the coffin in the first place. 'Chip Gainsborough was a shorter man.'

'Saw off his feet, then, for God's sake,' the Commander said.

'Yes, sir.'

'No! Stop! Please! No more! Leave him some dignity!' my mother cried.

'Now, now, sweet, gentle, lovely madam,' said the

46

Commander, trying desperately to be charming in spite of the dreadful atrocity he had just committed. 'Please do not concern yourself. My men have been trained to expect absolutely zero dignity should they attempt to undermine my authority.'

'Help!' screamed my mother, looking up at the sky. 'Someone, help us!'

Mike lined up a saw on poor Lyle's legs, and the teeth of the saw grazed his ankles and drew blood.

'Go on, then, Mike,' the Commander said. 'Saw them off!'

'Wait! Don't listen to him, Mike!' a voice cried.

It was Bud. He was standing with his legs astride like a cowboy, his pistol pointing at the Commander's head.

'Now, now, Bud. Whoa, there,' the Commander said. 'Easy, my deputy, my Number 2. Take it easy there, pal.'

'Drop the weapon, Commander!' yelled Bud. 'I'm serious! Game over!'

The Commander scowled, dropped the revolver, and put his hands on his head. 'Now, now, don't do anything stupid, Bud,' he said feebly, his voice cowering behind the barricade of his moustache. 'All I was doing was protecting the secrecy of our mission, and you know it.'

'Well, I think you went a little too far, don't you?' said Bud. 'I suggest you tell this terrified woman and her daughters what's going on. Tell them the truth about Chip!'

'Now, look here, Bud,' the Commander said. 'I was just

doing my job. Put the gun down now or you're going to regret this. Remember who's in charge.'

'Oh, I remember who's in charge, all right!' Bud said.

And, with that, he shot at the Commander's feet. The Commander danced to avoid the volley of bullets. He bucked and flinched and thrashed around like a fish on a hook before collapsing to his knees beside Lyle. He squeezed his hands in prayer until his knuckles went white.

'Now get up and tell them!' Bud said, when everything was quiet again. 'Tell them before it's too goddam late!'

'Okay, okay,' the Commander stammered, holding up his shaking palms. 'Okay, just cool it, for Chrissakes.'

He stood up slowly, mopped his brow with his sleeve, hoiked some phlegm from the back of his throat, and spat it on the ground. Bud stared at the glistening ball in disgust and then applied the same look to the Commander, who mumbled an apology and hastily scooped it up in a handkerchief and put it in his pocket.

'It's like this, ma'am,' the Commander said.

My mother's face was buried in her arms. She looked up. The tears on her cheeks were like slug trails.

'Ma'am, I am afraid I have been a little dishonest with you concerning the matter of the late Chip Gainsborough.'

'Keep going, Commander,' said Bud. 'Tell them everything.'

'There is no Chip Gainsborough,' the Commander whispered. 'And there never was.'

It wasn't easy to take in what the Commander had said. I felt for a moment like a quiz-show contestant who has drawn blank on the easiest question in the universe.

'There is no such person,' he continued. 'End of story. He is a fake, a nonentity. He was never part of our outfit. He never parachuted. He doesn't exist and never did.'

Aileen turned on Bud, tears streaming down her face. 'This can't be true, Bud,' she said. 'You said Chip was your best buddy. You grew up together. You dived for sand dollars!'

'I know,' he said. 'But it was all lies. I was just carrying out orders. You see, it's all part of the Commander's strategy, isn't it, Commander?'

'Yes,' said the Commander.

'Well, tell them, then, man!' screamed Bud.

'Our strategy, ma'am,' the Commander said, 'is that, upon landing on civilian property, we pretend we have lost a parachutist.'

'Pretend?' my mother said weakly.

'Correct. It makes us look more noble and heroic,' the Commander said. 'It gives us gravitas, and endears us to our hosts. It provides us with an aura of pathos, of bravery, of heroism, a chance to display our emotional range, our efficiency. It also means that the chosen family becomes more sympathetic to our cause. And so we pretend we lost a parachutist, and it helps us infiltrate a household much more easily.'

49

'But . . .' my mother stuttered, 'but, if what you say is true, that means you killed poor Lyle for no reason at all.'

'You are correct, ma'am,' the Commander. 'I did precisely that.'

'You killed him for nothing?'

'That's exactly what he did, ma'am,' Bud said. 'The Commander will go to any lengths to keep his mission a secret, won't you, Commander?'

The Commander nodded.

'What mission?' my mother whispered. 'What are you saying? Why did you come here, and what did you want from us?'

'Later, ma'am,' said Bud, pushing my mother aside. 'Right now I am going to avenge Lyle's death.'

He narrowed an eye and took aim at the Commander.

My mother turned away. Aileen slumped to her knees. I closed my eyes and tried desperately to think of something nice. And for some inexplicable reason what I thought of was my father reading me a story in bed. It was a story about camels. And it had a happy ending. It was about two camels who save their master in a sandstorm.

But Aileen screamed and the camels vanished from my head, and so did my father.

'Please, Bud!' she yelled. 'Whatever he's done, don't kill him. Two wrongs don't make a right. If you love me, no.'

'Love you?' screamed Bud. 'I don't love you, you whore. All I care about is this outfit and who leads it. Now, prepare to be dismissed, Commander!'

'Stop right there, Bud Mellors!' a voice boomed.

Bud froze.

'Who said that?'

'I did,' said the voice. 'If you kill the Commander, then I'll kill you! One move and you're dead!'

Bud turned to face the intruder.

It was Hank. The same Hank who had earlier brought back the pickup full of flowers, and his pistol was trained on Bud.

'You wouldn't,' whispered Bud.

'Try me,' said Hank.

'Ha!' Bud yelled nervously. 'You really think you could kill me, Hanky boy?'

'Oh, I'll wipe you out, all right,' Hank said calmly. 'You've always been an ambitious little bastard. You've always brown-nosed the Commander and had your eye on his job. And now you want to see him out of the way so you can take over.' He narrowed one eye and took aim. 'Well, I'm sorry, but that's not the way it's going to be, buddy boy! So long, for ever!'

'Wait! Stop right there, Hank! Stop, before I put a bullet in your skull!'

Hank jumped and turned around to face the music. One of his comrades had stepped forward. It was Pete.

Pete, who had blown the bugle so beautifully beside Chip Gainsborough's grave and had played his favourite song on my dad's guitar.

'If you kill Bud for killing the Commander, Hank, then the only flowers you'll be arranging are the ones on your grave.'

The men glanced at each other, apparently confused by the logic of who was going to kill whom, and who would end up dead and who alive. And then, suddenly, out of nowhere, and in a moment of what seemed to be sheer panic, all the other parachutists drew their pistols and within seconds there was earsplitting, splintering gunfire.

I threw myself to the ground and pretended to be dead. Bullets whizzed over my head. They shattered the windows of our house and ripped into the walls. Parachutists groaned as they fell heavily onto the ground around me. I closed my eyes tight and prayed that Aileen and my mother were doing exactly the same as me. Playing dead. Keeping out of the way.

And as I lay with my eyes shut tight I thought of the story about the camels again, and how well my father had done the voice of the camel. And then I imagined him sailing his boat directly against the wind somewhere near his house in San Francisco.

It seemed like for ever before the shooting stopped, but it might have been only a matter of seconds. I kept still. I waited. I held my breath and counted slowly to a hundred.

Then, ever so carefully, I lifted my head and turned my neck stiffly to the side.

No one was standing. Fifteen parachutists lay strewn on the ground. Pete had fallen over Greg's torso. Greg was lying with a hand in a pool of Hank's brains. Bud was sprawled at the feet of the Commander, whose back was peppered with bullet holes. The ground was stained with blood and gore. I could not see Mom or Aileen anywhere.

'Mom? Aileen? Aileen? Mom, are you there? Don't you leave me, too!' I yelled. 'Don't go and leave me.'

No one answered. All the blood drained out of my body and collected somewhere in my toes.

Finally, a voice said, 'Ryder, honey?'

My heart jumped in my rib cage as if I had been bitten. 'Mom!'

'I'm okay, darling,' she said. 'What about Aileen? Is Aileen okay?'

'I'm okay, you guys!' Aileen called. 'But, please, can you pick up their guns? I don't think I'll be able to get up until I know it's safe.'

'Stay where you are, girls,' my mother called.

She pulled herself to her feet and went tiptoeing among the bodies, foraging for the guns. She took them one at a time over to the house, wincing and holding them between two fingers, as if they were dead animals. She placed all the guns in a neat pile beside the front door. The last one she

collected was the Commander's. He had died holding on to it so hard that she had to pry his fingers off one by one.

'All right,' my mother said. 'It's okay, girls. I have disarmed every one of them. It's safe to get up.'

'Are you sure they're all dead?' Aileen asked.

'Positive,' said Mom.

The three of us stared at each other across the carnage. It felt as if a pulse were beating in my eyes. Later on, Aileen said she felt something like that, too. She said her eyes stepped out over the bodies first, and the rest of her came later. Anyhow, we ran into each other's arms and squeezed each other tightly.

'Thank God, my darlings,' my mother said. 'You're both alive.'

'Jesus Christ!' cried Aileen, bursting into tears. 'They're all dead! Fifteen of them, and look at the state of our house!'

She was right. There were holes in the walls, and several windows were smashed. The house seemed shaken and disturbed by what had happened.

'What are we going to do?' I said.

'The first thing is to keep calm,' my mother said. 'We have done nothing wrong, remember, and it is not our fault that we were invaded by these evil parachutists. Now, go upstairs and pack a bag,' she said. 'Be quick, and try not to forget anything.'

'Are we going away, Mom?'

'Yes, Ryder,' said my mother. 'You guessed it. We're going away. But first we have work to do.'

Aileen and I ran upstairs. Meanwhile, my mother packed food in a cooler and made a thermos of coffee. Then we went outside and ushered the chickens out of the coops into cages, and loaded them onto the back of the pickup.

'Now for the tough part,' my mother said.

We dragged each of the parachutists, one by one, across the ground. Aileen and I took a leg each and my mother gripped them by the wrists. We heaved them together into a pile, trying not to get blood on us, and as we did so we coated each parachutist in a layer of dust and dirt. Then I noticed something strange. Every dead parachutist had a smug kind of half smile and a look of extreme satisfaction on his face. It was as if by blowing each other to bits they had successfully completed their mission and everything had gone perfectly swimmingly and according to plan after all.

When, at last, the Commander had been reunited with his men, my mother took a can of gasoline from the shed and doused the pile of parachutists. She soaked their clothes, their hair, their feet, everything.

'Honestly,' my mom said, 'is it just me or do I seem to spend my whole life cleaning up after men?' She sighed and wiped her hands on a rag. 'Right, girls. That should just about do it. Now, ready to receive your instructions?'

'Go ahead, Mom.'

'Aileen, get in the pickup,' she said. 'Drive it a good

hundred yards away from the house and turn on the headlights. Ryder, untie the camels and secure them tightly to the side-view mirror. And make sure Nellie is with you, too.'

Aileen and I did as our mother said. We knew who was in command now.

'I don't believe this is happening,' Aileen said as we sat in the pickup stroking Nellie and telling her everything was going to be okay.

'Neither do I,' I said.

'Bud seemed so sweet,' she sniffed. And then she broke down in tears.

'Sis, he was an asshole,' I said, putting a comforting arm around her shoulder. 'They all were.'

In a few minutes, my mother closed the door of the house and locked it. Then she strode calmly over to the pile of bodies, struck a match and tossed it on, and made a dash towards us. Behind her, flames were already clawing at the sky.

'Well, that's that, then,' my mother said when she was safely in the driver's seat.

I unfolded a rug, and we laid it over our legs and turned off the headlights. We drank sweet coffee from the thermos and chewed on peanuts, as if we were at a drive-in movie.

'Pretty, isn't it?' said my mother. 'You can't beat a good honest fire on a summer's evening.'

'You sure can't,' said Aileen.

'Is everyone okay?'

'Yes,' I said. 'I guess. And the camels are fine.'

'Shaken, but okay,' said Aileen.

'What horrible men,' said Mom.

'They were despicable,' said Aileen.

'Pathetic,' I said.

My mother poured herself some more coffee.

'I guess they make your father seem like an archangel by comparison,' she said.

Aileen and I exchanged a look as my mother drummed her fingers on the steering wheel.

'Well, maybe not quite an archangel,' she said eventually.

Mom turned the key in the ignition and put the pickup into gear. We drove off slowly down the dirt road, the camels trotting alongside us.

'Where are we going, Mom?' I said.

She took a heavy breath.

'San Francisco, I guess,' she said.

I smiled and turned to look out the rear window. Sparks were pouring up into the black night sky. They soared up and up and up, and I followed them all the way with my eyes, until they flickered, and flared briefly, and then vanished.